DUSTSONG

LEN THE WANDERER

M. B. Heywood

This book is a work of antediluvian fantasy fiction. It is not intended as a factual account contradictory or supplementary to biblical and prehistoric accounts.

Cover art by Dusan Markovic. Licensed via BookCoverZone.

Published in the Commonwealth of Virginia, U. S. A., by Vaporous Realms Publishing LLC.

ISBN: 978-1-960180-04-9

Dustsong: Len the Wanderer / M. B. Heywood.

To Dad, who first introduced me to fantastical histories and imagined realms.

To Momma, who believed in this book before I wrote a word of it.

And to Havilah, who has made every word possible.

I love y'all.

TABLE OF CONTENTS

Chapter One:
The Hollow

Len pressed the last, round seed into its span-deep hole. With his digging blade, he scraped soil over the seed till it was buried under a little mound of earth. *I'm sure glad I tripped over that funny-looking rock 'ere yesterday.* The flat, slender length of stone had proven mighty useful for tending his growing things.

He stood for a look at the result of his afternoon's labor. A dozen small mounds of earth snaked around a patch of feathery grass he'd found. Podding plants grew taller near the spiky, kernelled barley-grass. Afore long, the pods and kernels alike would make for good eating.

"What goes, Len? Can we help?"

We? Len turned to find his little brother sitting atop a spindly-legged beast. The critter's giant horns, curled down to the sides of its head, resembled mouse ears.

"Why're you riding a sheep?" Len asked.

"It's not a sheep," Sceg insisted. "It's a bighorn."

Len scoffed. "Father says it's called a sheep. It's just a regular old mountain sheep."

"Father calls the critters whatever he wants. So can I!"

"Fine," Len said. "But why are you riding on its back?"

"So I can fetch you for supper."

"Wright almighty," Len huffed. "You sure take your time getting to the main thing."

"Sorry," Sceg said. He clambered down from the sheep as it munched on meadow grass.

Len shrugged. "Let's head back. I'm done here for today, anyhow. But you'd best keep that beast away from my garden."

"I'll try," Sceg replied cheerily. *He's naught if he isn't good-natured.* That was what their mother said. "I'll walk back so you aren't on your lonesome. Bighorns are faster than you'd reckon."

"Thanks," Len said. He stashed his digging blade under the fibrous cord that belted his britches. Sceg scampered over the piled-stone wall Len had built around his new garden to discourage rabbits and deer. The sheep followed close on Sceg's heels. All the critters seemed to like Sceg. *Same as they like Father.*

Len hadn't considered sheep. *Or goats.* He would have to build the wall higher on the morrow. And he'd do the same for all his other gardens, in case Sceg and his latest companion discovered those, too.

A stiff breeze whistled through the tall oaks. It tousled the boys' curly manes and set boughs a-waving. Meadow grasses fluttered and tickled Len's ankles. *The breath off Livyat's fangs.* That was what

Father called the ever-present wind whenever a gust damaged their cottage roof.

"The air is too sweet for that," Mother said, every time. "It must be the Wright giving us a whiff of the heaven-realm." *She says it a bit wistful-like.* It also helped dry their clean clothes on the line.

Len looked past the sheep's horns and Sceg's head, and over billowy treetops, at the Fangs. Tree cover, scraggly forevergreens mostly, continued a ways upslope of the hollow where Len and his family dwelt. The jagged mountainside rose higher yet, to snowcapped summits draped in cloud.

He imagined Livyat, the colossal she-snake, lunging skyward with her maw wide open. In that instant, the Wright had rained rock upon the Mother of Serpents, trapping her and her fangs forever under untold layers of earth.

Is she still awake in there? Can she see us right now, wading through the meadow? Len shivered.

They walked into a swathe of grass that swallowed Len to his waist and hid Sceg and his sheep nearly to their necks. Without warning, Sceg stopped short. "One day," he said, "I'll climb to the tip of the tallest Fang. Do you think I could see the Wright from up there?"

"Don't be a fool," Len replied. "You'd tucker out halfway to the top. Besides, the Wright wouldn't want the likes of us to trouble him."

Instead of being disappointed, Sceg took on a pondering air. *Like the light just afore dawn-break, Mother calls that look of his.*

They continued homeward. Len kept a wary eye on their silhouettes, stretched and twisted like demons. *If he's the sunrise, I suppose I'm the sunset shadow.*

The sheep trailed a few paces behind the brothers as they finished crossing the far meadow. They passed betwixt scattered stands of late-fruiting thorntrees. "I want to pick a few thornapples," Len said.

"But the bighorn can't follow us in," Sceg protested. "The brush is too thick. Anyhow, I helped Father bring in a basketful this morning."

"All right," Len relented. But he'd stop by tomorrow, for certain.

Clumps of pink and purple flowers welcomed them to the meadow nearest home. They moseyed past a family of sprightly deer some twenty paces off. When the lone yearling buck noticed them, he stopped and flaunted his improbably big antlers till the does and fawns had vanished into a nearby thicket.

"So, what name would you pick for a sprightly deer? A hairy hornbird?" Len teased. This earned a mock glare and playful shove from Sceg. The boys wrestled a bit while the sheep munched placidly on a sprig of purple flowers. Sceg managed to wriggle behind Len and wrap scrawny limbs around his neck and torso.

"Hey!" Len yelped. He tried not to sound as annoyed as he suddenly felt. "Let's get on home now. I'm hungry enough to eat a crag-goat."

"Me, too," said Sceg betwixt heaving breaths in Len's ear. "I'll race you!" he cried as he leapt off Len's back.

They ran flat-out into the open patch of bloodwoods on the far side of the meadow. With his longer stride, Len reached the woods first. Yet Sceg was lighter and surer of foot on the uneven, root-strewn ground betwixt the trees. By the time they spilled into a sunny glade, the brothers ran abreast.

A grey-daubed house of oaken poles and beams sat just across the way, in the middle of the glade. The cottage had a low roof, covered in bark shingles and thatch, and wide eaves. *It looks like it's wearing a funny sort of hat.* Len and Sceg didn't slow till they stood just outside the doorway, but the sheep joined them afore they'd caught a breath.

"You weren't kidding," Len wheezed. "That bighorn of yours is fast."

Sceg grinned. "Wait here," he told the critter. The sheep obliged by wandering over to their mother's earthen outdoor oven and nestling beside it. *Still warm.* That meant fresh-baked cakes. The boys ducked through the doorway shoulder to shoulder.

Mother sat on her stool at their squat-legged kitchen table, on the right-hand side of the front room. She wore her second-best summer tunic, the oak-leaf one, and had her wavy hair tied back. She was adding herbs to a bowl of what looked to be mashed roots. Assorted other vessels, and her cooking utensils, lay scattered across the table. Several small pots were filled with greens. But sure enough, a platter of cakes rested at her elbow.

"Almost ready, boys. Wash up."

Sceg obeyed, scurrying to the basin of water near the kitchen window. As soon as Mother's attention returned to her supper preparations, Len slunk over to the opposite side of the front room. Father reclined on his worn fiber mat. It was decorated with all kinds of critters and plants the boys had painted in an array of colors.

Father almost always looked out of the sitting-room window this time of day and watched the sun set through the trees. His expression now was thoughtful, like Sceg's sometimes. Len's father and little brother resembled each other in many a way, down to their ruddy-brown toes.

"You've been roaming too far," Mother commented from the kitchen. "What am I supposed to do if you cross paths with a wolf or a jackal out there on your lonesome?"

Be glad Sceg didn't get eaten, too. Len plopped down on the plain mat of brown and yellow fibers he'd woven himself.

"Easy, Lae," Father drawled. "Len's so shaggy, a wolf would probably mistake him for its cub."

"Don't humor him, Ghrem."

Father gave Len a weighing look. "From now on, little wanderer, mind you let me or your mother know where you're off to." Len grunted at the gentle chastisement.

Sceg joined them. His mat was frayed from all the times Mother had tried to scrub the critter smells out of it. "Father, guess what? I've got a new pet!"

"What is it named, mate?

"It's called a bighorn. That's its name."

Father looked a question at Len, who mouthed "sheep" behind Sceg's back and mimicked its curled horns with his fingers.

Father nodded and stroked his beard thoughtfully. "I reckon that's a fine name. Mayhap I should have thought of it myself." Sceg beamed. Len rolled his eyes.

"Tell us about some of the beasts you've named," Sceg pressed Father. "What was the funniest-looking one?"

Len scoffed. "You're always wanting to talk about that stuff."

"Well," Sceg said, a bit huffy for once, "what would you talk about?"

Len considered. He hated being put on the spot, so he asked the first question that popped into his head. "Does the Wright have growing things, and critters, up where he lives? In the sky-realm?"

Father blinked in surprise. "Well, now," he replied slowly. "That's quite a thing to ask. I can't say I rightly know. But if the Wright ever invites you up there, how about you find out for yourself. Then come back and tell me."

"Okay," Len said, disappointed. *That wasn't really an answer.*

Father turned his attention back to Sceg. "But as for the strangest critter I ever named, I may recall..."

Len left them talking and slunk over to the kitchen side of the room. Mother had already tidied the mess on the table into something resembling supper. She was setting a crock of thornapple paste beside the platter of cakes and noticed his interest.

"Wash," she ordered. This time he heeded her, afore swiping a cake and perching on his stool to the side of the table. He bit into it and took his time chewing. Without the thornapple dressing, the cake was bland, but that let him better appreciate its soft, slightly crumbly texture.

"You've got a storm brewing in that head of yours," Mother said, matter of fact. "What's amiss?"

"Sceg and Father are always going on about critters." *Excepting the two-legged sort, like me.* That didn't feel like the whole of his woes, but it was part.

"What would you rather talk about?"

Len tried not to be cross that she'd repeated Sceg's exact question. Instead, he gazed out the kitchen window. "Other places I've never been," he said. "Like the low country. And green things," he said. "Different kinds of trees and shrubs and such." *I reckon I'd find all kinds of interesting stuff growing outside our hollow.*

"Your father knows plenty about plants and trees," his mother suggested.

"No," Len said hurriedly. "I don't mean gathering things the way he does. I want to grow them in one spot, in gardens, so I can look at them and pick them for eating whenever I please."

What's that odd look on her face? He asked her as much.

She replied in a quiet tone, with a half-hearted smile. "I know a place you'd have liked, that's all."

Len decided to change the subject. "I want to know more about the Wright, too. Does he ever come visit our realm?"

Now Mother's face was downright troubled. *I'm sorry I asked.* But he munched the last bite of his cake in patient silence.

Right as he swallowed, she answered. "He used to. But folks made mistakes–" Her voice caught. "So now he doesn't come around." She sat back on her stool and called the others. "Supper's ready!"

Crumbs had stuck in Len's throat. He grabbed a chipped cup off the table and stood to fetch one of the water pouches hanging on the wall. "I'm not going to make mistakes," he declared after filling his cup and gulping a swig.

Mother almost responded but settled for exchanging a look with Father as he strode to the wash basin. *What's that about?*

Sceg stepped away from the basin and shook the water off his hands. With a mischievous grin and a chortle, he told Len, "Your face is a mistake."

Afore either of the grown folk could object, Len had flung his empty cup onto the table and was chasing his brother around the kitchen.

"Take it outside!" Father shouted.

Squealing like a squeaker-pig, Sceg bolted out the doorway. Len was right behind him.

"And then wash up again!" Mother yelled after the boys.

Len tackled his brother five paces from the cottage. They lay all a-tangle and laughing in the gathering gloam. The sheep observed from the shadows, without comment. All things considered, life under the sun, and under the Fangs, was good.

Chapter Two:
The Most Grievous Day

Hidden among forevergreens and thorntrees that scratched his bare arms and torso, Len watched his brother. Sceg stood silent in the meadow just below, where boulders of varied size seemed to weight the blanket of grass. Rocky outcrops punctured the ground cover up to shoulder height. A spread of flowers, comingled whiteapples and fireblooms, kept trying to draw Len's eye. *On a different day, I'd let them.*

The far side of the meadow ended in a shelf of rock and earth, but the grass grew right to the edge. That was where Sceg loitered, with the cool, dry wind lapping against his cloak. His flock of bighorns had scattered behind him to graze. With his back to Len, Sceg leaned on his sheep-herding crook and looked south. *Taking in the view. With that pondering look on his face, no doubt.*

The view was familiar after thirty-odd years living in the Fangs. Yet it remained worth contemplating. The mountainous, mist-shrouded remnants of the battle where time began, betwixt Livyat and the Wright, sprawled across the landscape in all directions, excepting east. There the Fangs simply ran to ground in the wastes.

But I'm not here to appreciate the Wright's handiwork. Len slid down a short, grass-tufted slope into the meadow. Though he hadn't noticed the sharp rock edges that scraped his feet and bit his calves, he didn't much care. The nicked and bruised flesh only deepened his agitation.

Len picked himself up. Feeling bold as summer thunder, he trod through pale green, knee-high blades. He was angrified and didn't bother keeping it from his face. A bighorn scampered out of his path.

It was no surprise Sceg heard him coming. "You were wanting to meet me here this morning." He half-turned toward Len. "I didn't think I'd be first to arrive. Midday will be on us soon."

He wasn't here first, any more than he was first out of Mother's womb. But Len didn't trouble to correct him. "Hello, brother," he said. Half a dozen paces from Sceg, he slowed to a halt. "Guess where I've been?"

Now Sceg turned fully to face him, but he didn't reply. Len answered his own question. "I took a gift to the lord of the sky-realm."

Len paused again. Sceg still didn't take the bait. *I reckon we've had this conversation afore.*

"He never showed," Len told his brother. He could hear the vein of spite running through his own fluster. In the back of Len's mind, Father's voice chastened him to watch his tone. *"We owe the Wright our respect. And our fear."* Len ignored the warning.

"The Wright couldn't be bothered, I reckon," he snarked instead. Too riled to stay put, he took a few erratic steps closer to Sceg. They'd been of a height since they were full-grown, but otherwise, their resemblance had always been tenuous. *As Mother's pleased to remind us. The dawn-break child with hazel eyes. And the brown-eyed dusk child.*

"So, then I set fire to my gift," he told Sceg. "It was the first and best of what I harvested this seven-day past. And still he didn't show. Not one word. Not a sign."

His brother studied him with infuriating calm.

"It took hours to burn the sheaves of wheat and barley. Unnatural long, I'd say. And even the berries didn't go up straightaway. Why do you think that is, brother?"

Sceg's answer, when it came, sounded tired. "I couldn't say for certain."

Len seethed. "We both know why. It's because he didn't want them. He never wants what I offer."

In that grating way of his, Sceg tilted his head and hesitated, as if he had words to speak but insisted on pondering them to a pulp first.

"What, naught to say?" Len knew his smile didn't go any further than the corners of his mouth. Neither his heart nor his eyes felt it in the slightest. The ire in his tone was ugly, but he couldn't keep it inside. *I've done that for too long, to no avail.* Today, he'd loose all the things choking his soul.

Finally, deliberate-like, Sceg broke his silence. "You did the same as always and expected something new to follow. I don't know what's got you perplexed."

"It perplexes me every time," Len retorted, "that the best fruits of my troublesome toil are scorned, while he gladly accepts a few scraps of your sheep-meat. All that's required of you is to brood up here on your bony rump all day."

Sceg shrugged lightly. "He is a lord of living, breathing things. Mayhap he wants to be honored with the blood of life." Half a breath later, afore Len could protest, Sceg added, "Or it's the drudging way you go about giving him gifts. What lies unseen in your soul. Because his realm is one of unseen things."

At that, Len threw up his hands. "The way I do it? If the Wright doesn't care for the taste of food that grows in the earth, then he ought to tell me to my face," he growled. "He should show himself and talk to me direct." *Like he used to talk to Father and Mother.* "Instead, he ignores us. You'd think we were barbarians."

Sceg was clearly unconvinced by this course of reasoning, and he sniffed contemptuously at Len's mention of the valley-dwellers. He'd been more curious, upon a time, but lately it was all about those confounded sheep. *I'm the only one who cares a whit anymore about goings-on beyond the hollow.* Father whiled away his time in the woods, picking berries and talking to wild critters. Mother pined quietly for the home she and Father had lost in somewise, afore they built the cottage.

Len wanted to explore the earthly realm and meet the sundry folk who must dwell on it. He itched to know what sorts of plants grew out there and how to make them grow better. *I want to know how things are different and how they fit together.* Meanwhile, Sceg didn't care. Len's brother was busy getting lost in himself.

When Sceg spoke again, Len could tell his brother's patience was thinned. "Did you subdue Livyat? Did I? If the Wright keeps his own counsel and doesn't ask what we think reasonable, I'm not sure who we are to complain."

"We're not lords, no, but have we wronged him?" Len fumed. "I know Mother or Father mayhap gave him some offense. But I don't recall offending anybody, let alone the storm-tamer who bested Livyat. Sometimes, I wonder if we're not punished for our folks' errors."

Sceg rested both hands and his bearded chin atop his crook. "If we suffer because of each other, sometimes, that's the way of the realm under the sun. If a beast of my flock wanders, and a prowler-cat attacks and devours another sheep while I search for the first, it can't be helped."

Len scoffed. "Mayhap it can't be helped after the fool thing's been digested already. But it's your fault for letting the one wander and the other be eaten, isn't it, now." It wasn't a question.

With a shrug, Sceg said, "You can twist the matter however you choose." Then he added, testily, "Consider, brother, if the Wright isn't just ruler of the blue sky. Or of the yellow sun or the green earth. I reckon he means to be lord of you and lord of me."

Len took a menacing step closer to Sceg, putting them in arm's reach. A mist, dark enough to obscure his own soul from view, had settled over his mind. *It's uncommon hard to think straight.* Though he gave his head a quick shake, it failed to part the fog inside.

"Isn't that a boon for you?" Len sneered, returning the conversation to more comfortable soil. "The Wright smiles on your labor, if your daydreaming among beasts can be called that. I work twice as hard as you, at the least. I get dirt under my nails. How often do you break a sweat?"

So consuming was the glower Len fixed on Sceg, he could hardly see his brother anymore. "And my gifts are despised. They come from the same dust as Father and Mother, but it seems they're worth naught. What's so special about your fool critters?"

"You'll never see why," Sceg answered evenly, "because you think only of what you're owed."

Then his gaze took on a regretful aspect, near apologetic, at odds with the sharpness in his voice. "I reckon it's time you leave, Len. Climb the Fangs as high as you can and try to take from the Wright what you think is proper. Or else head downslope and live among the barbarians who fascinate you so. Grow your gardens. Be contented."

Now Sceg's features hardened to match his tone. "But whichever way you choose, get yourself gone from here. I don't rightly know why you wanted to see me, or what you expect, but let me have my peace."

Len's cheeks were hot with indignation. When he found words again, they came out wintry. "Well, I surely didn't bring you here to yammer all day." The words flowed unabated. "Mayhap you should be the one to leave, Sceg."

Back in the day, they'd oft provoked one another, in a playful manner. *Neither of us is jesting now.* Somewhere along the way, things betwixt them had stopped growing the way they should. Now they'd gone awry beyond recourse.

But that wasn't my doing. After all, Len was dutiful. He honored the Wright, no matter what his brother said, and he minded their parents well enough. Len was the eldest and deserved some respect himself. Yet the Wright favored Sceg and his presumptuous airs. Sceg, who was oblivious or unfeeling as to the hurt Len felt. If not for his brother, Len could live peaceably with himself.

He's in my way.

That notion caught aflame the darkling mist inside Len. The last semblance of control slipped from his grasp. He shoved Sceg.

Unprepared, his brother stumbled backward. He retained his grip on his crook with one hand but nearly lost his balance on the uneven ground. They looked at each other in startlement for a few heated, hasty heartbeats. Len blinked in the sunny glare off the mountain haze.

Then, with an enraged bellow, Len rammed Sceg like a maddened crag-goat. Sceg made a clumsy effort to block his brother with his crook, which only angrified Len further. This time, he knocked Sceg down, into the grass.

Sceg had dropped his crook and let it lie as he clambered to his feet. Len saw the fire in his brother's countenance, now, that he felt in his own. With no other forewarning, except the slightest shift in posture, Sceg threw himself at Len. Their collision knocked the breath clear out of Len's lungs.

The brothers grappled awkwardly. In their fierce, grunting exertions, they staggered to and fro. Neither gained the upper hand for more than an instant. Len couldn't focus his eyes proper. Only dimly was he aware how near the precipitous edge of the meadow their tussle brought them.

I'm starting to fade. How long had they continued in this furious, pitiful manner? Afore he could deplete himself entirely, he mustered all his might into one burst and tried to force Sceg to the ground.

The surge of strength must have caught Sceg unawares, and they must have been closer to the mountain face than Len realized. The next thing Len knew, Sceg hung off a ledge, from his waist up, over a sheer drop. It was several dozen paces to the brush-covered ledge below. Len strained to hold his brother by the legs to keep him from tumbling into space.

Tears and sweat streamed together down Len's cheeks. "Just tell me true," he gasped, "why the Wright loves you more." Sceg made no reply save for a dry, wheezing sob.

Lost for any other words, Len hauled him back from the brink to the safety of the grass and helped him upright. Noticing Sceg's sluggish, tremulous movements, he made a point of placing himself betwixt his brother and the cliff. *Not that I'm in much better shape.*

Then Sceg said something. He had to attempt it a couple of times afore his voice broke through his labored breathing. "Serpents take you, Len. You're only dust to me."

With neither thought nor hesitation, Len pulled his digging blade from his belt and clobbered his brother across the face. Sceg tumbled backward to the earth. A sickly crack sounded, and he emitted a little cry.

What just happened?

After Sceg lay still and silent for a prolonged moment, Len moved forward warily. A gash from the stone blade oozed across Sceg's terribly bruised brow. *But that doesn't account for all this blood.* The back of his brother's head had landed on a small outcrop less than a span high. Red wetness pulsed and pooled on the rock; it traced the imperfectly hewn edges and trickled to the ground.

Sceg worked his mouth without speaking. His yellowish green eyes blinked wide and fearful. Len collapsed to his knees in horror. Though he was doused in sweat, his blood coursed cold. *What am I supposed to do?*

In a rising panic, he asked Sceg. "What's going on? Speak to me!" For good measure, he added, "I'm a fool–I know it." *Naught but a fool. What have I done?* He hadn't meant for this. *That doesn't count for aught, does it?*

At last, his brother made an utterance. Len leaned closer to hear.

"Sleep," Sceg mumbled. "Rest awhile." Then all the tension in his features dissipated. His whole body relaxed, as if in slumber, except that his eyes stared heavenward, unblinking and distant.

Len wept. He wailed, and he pleaded. He demanded the unseen-folk help him. And he cried for the Wright, reckoning that the lord of the skies might in somewise revive the one he favored. "If you love him so, then mend him! Put the breath and blood of life back in him!"

There was no reply. No help arrived, nor any hopeful sign. He screamed at the Fangs, keenly aware he sounded more like a beast than a man. *We were fighting like lesser critters, too.* Now Sceg lay slain and drained of life, like so much carrion.

A lull in his despair, born of exhaustion, gave him the chance to stand and look about. His knees and calves griped painfully. *How long have I been here?* The sheep had scattered without a trace, but the sun wasn't long in its descent.

What now? It was the same earthly realm all around him, yet changed beyond revocation. The world felt different. *I'm ruined.*

For certain sure, Len couldn't go back home. Nor could he remain anywhere near the sky-realm, lest he wander into the wrathful clutches of the Wright. After this most grievous day, the only choice left him was the low country.

What will I need? My cloak. A water pouch or three. Food. My– Belatedly, he realized he was still gripping his digging blade. He raised his hand to discard it, but paused at the last instant.

I have to hide Sceg. To keep the critters from him.

Len stuck the length of stone back in his belt. Once Sceg was buried, he could slip into the hollow and gather the few things he needed. *After dark. While Father and Mother sleep.* Then he'd make his way downward, Wright help him. *Except he won't.*

Chapter Three: DOWNWARD

Len bolted upright to see moonlight glancing off low-lying clouds above and the boulders strewn about. Crimson-tinged memories of cold flesh and lifeless eyes dissipated quick with the anxious rhythm of his heart and a few gasps of cool mountain air. Half-dried sweat stuck to his neck and brow.

After a few moments, his waking senses washed the creeping rivulets of blood fully from his mind. *Sceg.* Reverberations of his brother's voice, twisted in anguish, receded. Len's vision was free again of murky waves without end, monstrous beasts big as hills, and folk clad like songbirds carrying on in ways he couldn't comprehend. It was him alone in the night with the sound of his own deep, steadying breaths.

Clambering to his feet, Len pulled his goat-hair cloak, his only garb besides his britches, snug about his shoulders. The knee-high grass wasn't too dewy this far downslope. *Not like home. In the hollow, I could wash myself head to toe with damp grass.* When these blades lightly brushed his calves, they tickled more than itched.

He was fully awake now. *Gone from one nightmare to another.* Every night so far, the dreams had come for him, and they were all kinds of disturbing. Some were beyond his ken, while others he comprehended too well.

It's the Wright. He's fixed to punish me whenever I sleep. The sky-lord might be to blame, or mayhap not. It didn't much matter, as Len couldn't stop the nightmares from coming. *I can't stop running, either. I can't change what I've done.*

Down here the insects were louder than back in the hollow. Day and night, it kept him unnerved a touch. *But there are worse things.*

As if demons had heard his thought, an eerie howl pierced the nocturnal hum that swelled all around. It raised hairs on his arms and turned his spine chill. Several answering yelps sounded along this stretch of the mountain, upslope as well as down.

Dogs of some sort. Len only knew the little grey wolves his father favored, that hunted rabbits and crag-goats in the forevergreen thickets. Given the echoing nooks and crannies in the mountainside, and sporadic tree-cover, it was hard to say how close or far the beasts might be.

The canine cries continued. There seemed more yearn in them than mourning or menace. *Human-folk aren't the only critters that get lonesome for kin, I suppose.* All the same, he squatted and scanned the dark warily. His fingers searched the flattened grass where he'd slept. *I know it's here.* When he felt the long, slender stone, he grasped it tight in one hand. *Not that it would save me from a pack of hungry beasts.*

He didn't move a twitch as the howls moved off north, fading until they stopped abruptly. *They must have found each other.* At least they weren't cats. A spotted prowler-cat was big enough to eat a goat in one sit, but it never let human-folk see it till it wanted to be seen.

Time to get going. Though the clouds hung low, there was no fog nearabout to keep him from predators' eyes. But that also meant he could see danger coming tolerably well. If naught else, it was better to start the day early, and a little tired, than to risk drifting off again. *No sense wandering into another dream.*

"Serpent spawn!" he hissed. He clapped a palm to his forehead. His brow felt smooth and cool to the touch, but for an instant, he would have vowed someone was carving into it. *With a firebrand.* The burning subsided almost as quick as it had come and left a raw, dull itch in its place.

That was the worst yet. The inexplicable head pains that came and went, in odd moments, were altogether more worrisome than nightmares or ravenous critters. Either demons were up to something or the Wright was. Len wasn't sure whose attentions he desired least.

In silence and haste, he gathered his few belongings to depart. He wet his throat from one of his water pouches afore he slung it, and the two empty ones, across his chest. His food supply, comprising almonds and hard cakes wrapped in large leaves, were stashed in the deep pockets Mother had sewn into his cloak. To be safe, he felt the pockets anyway to make sure naught had fallen out. He kept his digging blade in hand.

As prepared as could be, he crept wide of the rock ledge a few paces from where he'd lain. Carefully, he picked his way downslope by the light of the moon. Whenever the going got tricky, he dug his stone blade into the earth to steady himself and felt things out with his free hand or his rough-hewn feet. *To think I nearly left my blade behind.*

Considering that the doggish-sounding critters had headed north, he descended in a southerly fashion for a while. *But always downward.* It was the only path left him.

Was that mist in his eyes? *Fool.*

Len meandered betwixt piles of boulders and stands of gnarled thorntrees. He avoided drops of middling height that he might have attempted in daylight. A lone tree in the near distance–*bloodwood?*–caught his notice. When he approached the tree, he recognized the silhouette of a crag-goat by its base. He changed course sharply, from southwest to due west. *"Let slumbering goats lie," Father always says. And he knows his critters.* Crag-goats might be prey for some beasts, but with legs thick as saplings and horns able to crack rock, Len would be more the fool to wake one.

A little while later, with the first hint of predawn pink in the sky, he found himself in a predicament. There was no way forward, as best he could tell, aside from a difficult slope over thrice his height. It scarcely offered a ledge for footing or stray root to grab hold of. Feeling too ornery to double back, he scrabbled downslope with a fair amount of trouble and frequent use of his digging blade.

At the bottom, after dusting himself off, Len looked up in the waning night to see two glinting eyes. They were deep-set in a furred face behind a snub snout and massive jaws. The beast standing on a boulder a few paces off wasn't quite feline or ursine, but more like the biggest wolf he'd ever come across, with a touch of cat and bear in the mix. Its mane ran in a comb along its back. *This is what Father meant by a mountain jackal.*

The jackal growled low and long. It hunkered down as if contemplating a pounce. Len's instincts were torn betwixt moving to a crouch and setting his stance wide for a tussle. *Steady. No sense provoking the beast.* Sure as snakes slithered, this was one critter he couldn't outrun.

Len didn't budge, but his muscles were tense enough to snap. He braced his mind and felt fleeting appreciation for the digging blade gripped tight in his left hand. It let him feel less defenseless than he reckoned he was.

The jackal began to lunge; the pitch of its growl rose of a sudden. Lips curled back from knife-like teeth. Len flinched and started to shift his left foot for better traction.

Then the beast froze. One of its forelegs was already midair. With a whimper, it drew itself back onto the boulder. Afore Len could take a full breath, it had slunk off to the south.

Bewildered, Len waited while the fog cleared from his mind. After a spell, his heart gave up trying to escape his chest, and he closed his gaping mouth. *Did it smell something? A spotted prowler?* Mayhap it hadn't sensed a critter at all but a demon or another of the unseen-folk.

He set out to the north and west, with the aim of putting as much downslope distance as he could betwixt him and the jackal. *Afore it changes its mind and comes back with its kin. Or whatever scared it off comes looking for me instead.*

By the time dawn arrived for true, Len had exerted himself and his mind near to exhaustion. He reckoned no critter or spirit was in pursuit anymore, if ever it was. *I ought to find a comfortable spot to rest and breakfast.* His flesh and neck hairs were still a-tingle, but it was likely just the lingering effects of his near escape. *The fact I'm not tore to pieces and resting in that great dog's stomach.*

Yet such reasoning failed to quell his agitation. Try as he might, Len couldn't quite shake the feeling that some critter had eyes on him.

Past a tenacious scrub-oak on its grassy perch, he slid down a short, sharp dip that set his water pouches bouncing. At the bottom, he caught his breath and scanned the slope ahead. The mountainside was gentling, the grass brightening, and the clumps of trees thickening. *Are those fruiting trees?*

Closer inspection proved it so. He paused for a respite under the diminutive pear trees, which had taken up residence on a flat, especially green tract of mountainside. For the next while, he plucked the more promising specimens, munching on some and stowing others in his pockets. Once he tore through the tough, yellowish skin, the underripe flesh beneath was the best thing he'd tasted in days. A brisk breeze likewise refreshed his soul. The nightly refrains of insects had given way to chittering birdsong.

Once he'd eaten his fill of pears, Len sat himself under one of the trees and splayed his bare legs on the lush grass. He reclined against the slender trunk and rummaged in his pockets for a leaf-wrapped packet of almonds. When he found it, he took his time cracking each nut in his palm and chewing it slowly, one after another.

The undulating valley below was visible now, save for a few patches of fog hanging over the near foothills. The northern bank of the blue-tinted river, in the shadow of the Fangs, was verdant. On the far, southern bank, pale greens and yellows ceded gradually to earthy tones and a series of rounded, dusty ridges. Beyond those, he couldn't see. To the west, the valley wound its way into the furthest reaches of the Fangs. To the east, the river bled itself dry in an empty, arid wasteland.

Though he'd beheld the valley afore, it was never from so close a vantage. The slope below soon swept upward again, into the nearest line of hills. Thorntrees and shrubby oaks were ever-present, same as upslope. Taller oaks and bloodwoods, likewise familiar, abounded here. In place of forevergreens, Len discerned stands of long-limbed trees he'd seldom encountered. *The proud ones whose leaves bare tiny teeth. The full, shapely ones with leaves like hands.*

Movement caught Len's eye. He wasn't the only critter appreciating the plant life. Thirty paces southwest, a sprightly buck-deer was nibbling on barley-grass in a wide meadow. It swiveled its little head his way, remarkably quick for those prodigious antlers. After meeting his stare from afar, or so Len imagined, it darted off.

For the first time since he'd paused by the pear trees, Len had the vague sense of an unseen watcher. *The deer?* But he reckoned he knew the feel of a critter spying on him, and this was different. *Livyat?*

Though he scanned his surroundings in every direction, and peered around the tree at his back, he saw scant out of the ordinary. There was only a short-muzzled bear, grey-furred and exceedingly round. The self-absorbed critter troddled past him, east to west, a hundred paces off.

Beyond the bear, betwixt the bottom of the mountain slope and the rise of the foothills, sunrays caught a silvery glint through tendrils of morning mist. *Water–Wright be thanked. Not that the sky-lord cares for my gratitude.* Len had crossed no streams going on three days now, which meant he'd be licking dew off grass this time on the morrow if he couldn't refill his water pouches.

Not relishing that prospect, he rewrapped and repacked the remaining unshelled almonds. Then he hastened toward the distant shimmers. A hawk gliding overhead reminded him to take his digging blade in hand again. *Seeing as I'm more liable to find beasts or barbarians at a watercourse. It's naught to do with the Fangs' prying eyes and unsettledness.* Even so, mayhap those wouldn't follow him into the bottomlands. He wished he could be surer.

A pair of sprightly doe-deer dashed out of the way as he approached the streambank. When he didn't give chase, they stopped short. The critters kept a leery eye on him but returned to grazing.

Len knelt on the bank to fill his pouches. He willed the amicably gurgling water to carry off some of his apprehension. *It's taking the edge, leastways.* The clear creek was only a few strides across, and its bed was clearly visible. *Nowhere for Livyat's demons to hide.* Much as he'd have liked to linger, Len waded to the far side afore any critters less benign than the deer got a thirst.

The first foothill, part of an east-west ridge, had sparsely distributed trees that made for an easy ascent. Cresting it, Len was glad he'd kept on. A view of the world from mountain heights, grand as it might be, couldn't compare to the vibrant scene before him now. Standing just inside the bounds of the valley, he took in the full breadth of the rolling landscape. Near the horizon, a dark tree-line marked the north bank of the great river. Open woodland, and groves of fruit- and nut-bearing trees, filled the foreground. Across flowering fields, a dozen kinds of grasses swayed in the wind. In the middling distance, herds of hulking, long-horned bovines loitered on hillocks and hillsides. *Aurochs. Breaking their own fast.* Father never paid Len much mind, but he'd given him names for many a critter he'd never seen afore.

Imagine what sort of garden a body could grow down here. For the first time in a goodly spell, light bloomed in his heart. But just as quick, the weight of the digging blade in his left hand brought on a soul aching. He missed the gardens he'd left behind, where he'd bided so many of his days. *Always by my lonesome.* Mother never outright discouraged his yearn to sow and cultivate, but nor could she muster real enthusiasm. *She never came to visit my growing things. And Father chose not to notice aught I did.*

With a deep breath, more resigned than liberated, he started down the south side of the hill. A second, brush-strewn line of foothills lay beyond. He climbed the next hill, to the scrub-oak thicket at its summit. It wasn't till Len rounded the brambly mess at the thicket's edge and peeked over the rise that he saw the other folk.

Chapter Four:
Rash and Regretful Acts

Startlement and dread whelmed Len's senses over. *Snake spit.* There were three barbarians, all of them men with dark hair and beards akin to his. Yet they dressed more like his mother: each was clothed in a hide tunic that covered neck to knee. The strange folk were laughing and picking pomegranates from a grove betwixt the second and third lines of hills.

Where do I hide? When he was a child, and a pale-skinned hunter had happened on the hollow, Father hid them all deep in the woods. But if Len hid in the thicket and the barbarians came up here, he'd be trapped.

I could run. Years back, when ranging high in the Fangs, Len had stumbled into a camp of yellow-haired folk. *It was the crag-goat's fault. Sceg was with me that time.* The knot in his gut cinched tighter. They'd fled home with their tails betwixt their legs. But now Len had ventured into others' country. *I could run from this lot and into worse.* He squeezed his digging blade tight. A shiver ran the length of his spine.

Belatedly, he saw one of the men below was pointing at him. Like lightning in a hurry, Len sprang into motion. He hurtled himself downhill, straight back the way he'd come. It required every scrap of his fear-heightened focus to keep from tripping over his feet or the brush, or slipping on the uneven terrain.

Retreating up the first hill, back toward the place he'd crossed the stream, would leave him exposed to plain sight. *Presuming they're after me.* Unsure what to do next, he let his feet do the deciding. As soon as he reached the bottom of the grade, he veered left without missing a step. He pressed northward, up the narrow slit of a valley betwixt the first and second ridges.

He spared a brief glance over his shoulder and glimpsed one of the men on the hilltop he'd just vacated. *Where are the others? How much trouble do they reckon I'm worth?* He supposed they couldn't know where he'd come from, or why. But even so, there was no telling what they'd do if they caught up with him.

Confused snatches of fretful reason and unreason pursued him as surely as the barbarians' gruff shouts. It was a breathy speech that sounded like gibberish to Len. *How in Livyat's lair am I to live in a world full of these folk?*

Ahead was a stream—a different spot on the selfsame creek he'd already crossed. There were breaks in the ridges to either side that he hadn't seen afore. *That's where the stream winds through the hills. On its way west to the river.*

The barbarians' shouts dwindled in his mind. The need to put distance betwixt himself and any other soul, every other soul, swallowed up his focus. He poured sweat, hot and cold at once, from head to toe. *If only I could get over the creek, I'd be safe enough.* Mayhap it was true, mayhap not, but the notion kept him going. Then he'd start for the stream after that, with all his might. He'd keep on north, across the hills and waterways, and never look back. *I'll get lost in the rocks and the woods till no living being can ever find me.*

Len's pounding heart dropped into his gut when a man sprang from the creek bank ahead to his left, not ten paces away. At a glance, he appeared to be of an age with Len. But the stranger was shorter of stature and paler of skin, and had a longer beard. In both hands, the man gripped a wrist-thick tree branch hewn to a point. *I'd hoped they weren't hunters. I reckon I'm the quarry.*

When Len stopped short, Long Beard slowed to a cautious advance. The man finally paused five paces off but kept the sharp end of his hunting stick aimed Len's way.

Then he tucked the spear under one arm. With the other hand, he alternated tugging at the shoulder of his tunic and jabbing a finger at Len. The barbarian's insistent babble sounded like wind whipping around the mouth of a mountain cave.

None of this eased Len's worry one bit. "You want my cloak?" he asked the barbarian.

Long Beard appeared just as perplexed at hearing him speak as the other way round. For the space of a labored breath, Len considered tearing off his garment and throwing it at the other man. *If only to distract him so I can get free. I'd rather be naked than keep this up.*

When their gazes caught, he glimpsed menace lurking under the man's skittering surface. Len recollected the fog such a mix of feelings brought. *A soul like that is prone to rash and regretful acts.* Unbidden images of Father and Mother's forlorn faces, bearing the betrayal and disbelief he hadn't waited to witness, surfaced in his mind. *Don't test or trouble this man. Escape.*

A shout from the hillside behind and to his left dispersed all other thoughts. Len backed away from Long Beard and turned to find another man, grey-bearded to his waist, shuffling rapidly downhill. Old Beard wielded a sturdy staff. By instinct, Len raised his stone blade in his defense.

"No!" thundered a voice in his head. It was his own, in somewise, yet arose from elsewhere. He lowered his blade and ran from both barbarians. He headed back eastward, betwixt the first and second ridges. There was no thinking his way out of this mess. His thoughts raced quicker than his bruised, blistering feet, till he settled on one: *keep running.*

Such a tumult was his mind, and so bright was the risen sun, Len didn't notice the pocket-like depression in the hillside to his right till he was almost upon it. Only then could he see the third barbarian, who leapt from the dip and planted himself square in front of Len. Like the first, this man carried a pointed stick, but he was clearly younger. as well as rounder and ruddier of face. From the agitated way the youth brandished his spear, he was also more terrified than his companions.

Like the yearling bear. He'd once come face to face with an excitable young bear a ways outside the hollow. He knew he couldn't pass it or outrun it. For lack of options, he'd rushed it head on. Unnerved, the critter had shown him its backside.

Afore he could reconsider, Len threw himself at Young Beard in frenzied desperation. He yelled wordlessly and waved his stone blade with abandon for added effect. And the brazen charge succeeded. The youth flinched and lowered his spear in fright.

But with two paces left betwixt them, Young Beard steadied himself. Instead of cowering or turning heel, the younger man dropped to the ground on both knees and whipped the spear up.

Too great was Len's momentum now to avoid Young Beard's flailing attempt at self-preservation. He tried to pivot anyway, twisting his body sideways and shifting his weight hard to the right. The upward sweep of the sharpened branch grazed his cloak. As Len lost his balance and fell, the spear-point pierced his shoulder through the goat hide.

Pain blossomed from his neck to his arm. He tumbled to the ground and rolled onto his back. Absently he realized he'd dropped his digging blade. All he could manage was to look skyward and wait for one of the barbarians to set upon him.

No such thing happened. Len mustered the strength to prop himself on his forearm. The slight pull on his injured shoulder produced a fearsome kind of hurt. It faded the instant he absorbed the horror before him.

Young Beard still knelt on the ground nearby. Everything else was changed. Shock had replaced fear in the youth's wide eyes. His gaping expression was fixed like a carving in wood. White light seemed to glow within his chest, even through his clothes. In mere moments, the light grew red and warm enough to waft heat Len's way. Flames burst through Young Beard's tunic. They blackened the beast hide and danced in the morning air until, finally, the burning body crumpled into the tall grass.

Only then did Len heed the woman standing just behind the lifeless barbarian. Arms extended in front of her, she held an enormous knife of flame and light. Never had Len imagined such a being. Dark, red-tinted locks framed angular features. Her skin was the hue of pine, more akin to the barbarians than to Len. *If folk were wrought from trees, she'd be fashioned from a willow.*

The willowy woman glided over Young Beard's body. The flames rising from the corpse gave off no smoke and seemed not to affect her, or to catch the grass alight. She glared down her nose at Len. “Get you up,” she demanded. Her tone exuded annoyance at odds with the singsong cadence of her speech.

Len didn’t dare contend with her. He clasped his hand over the blood-matted goat hair on his throbbing shoulder and scanned about briefly. Long Beard and Old Beard had made themselves scarce. With grunts and groans, he pulled himself awkwardly to his feet afore returning his full attention to the woman.

He found the scene transformed again. Her eyes had gone as unnaturally white as her sleeveless tunic. The garment was seamless, excepting a thin line of gold trim, and showed nary a wrinkle. Afore Len could blink, in one fluid motion, the woman brought her arms to her sides and extinguished her fiery blade without a trace. Behind her, the landscape was bathed in an unearthly haze. It was a dense sort of mist that seemed to emit its own ethereal light. *Am I awake?*

At first, Len reckoned he only imagined bloody spots in the snowcaps of the great Fangs. *Mayhap I split my head and the wound’s a-drip.* Then the deep red dots took the form of fireblooms. *Like the ones in the meadow that day.* The dots became a stream of crimson flowers cascading down the mountainsides. He had half a mind to rub this dream from his vision, if he could, yet he resisted. The strange image held his eyes captive.

A wind blew down from the red-stained mountain. *Too warm to be coming from the north as it is.* This uncanny current of air bore a voice his way. It was a whisper that filled his skull fit to burst. He'd heard it afore. *And I thought I'd heard the last of it.* As usual, it posed a question.

WHERE IS HE?

"How should I know?" Len lied without thinking. His voice sounded hoarse and wavered with a dreadful tremor. "It's all I can do to look after my own self." He stared as the red streams trailed halfway downslope.

Lying to the voice was a fool thing. *He never seems to ask aught out of ignorance.* A lord of the unseen would know exactly what had transpired and why he had left the Fangs. But Len couldn't bring himself to give the truth words. That would lend it credence. The woman's white eyes looked through him, and Len's through her.

When the voice responded, it was no longer a whisper. *THE EARTH LAMENTS!* It was so loud, Len supposed his head would explode. His knees tried to buckle beneath him, but some unseen spirit locked them up tight. The flow of tears down his cheeks mimicked the bloody rivers of fireblooms, which gathered strength on their serpentine course into the valley.

YOUR LABOR IS CURSED. THE GROUND HERE IS AWASH IN BLOOD AND WILL YIELD YOU NAUGHT, WANDERER, FROM THIS DAY FORTH!

"No," Len said, his pitch tense and rising. He wept harder and repeated himself at a shout, more indignant than pleading. "No! Did I deny you some respect or honor due? What instruction did I ignore? I paid my tribute!" *So why am I spurned, time and again? Why am I alone punished?*

"Turn a blind eye to me!" Len cried. "Or expel me from the hollow and from Livyat's fangs! But don't take the soil from me!" *Don't rob me of the growing things. They're all I have left.*

THEY ARE NOT YOURS, the voice said plainly, once more a whisper so resounding it could swallow up the sky-realm.

"But I'll starve," Len protested, "or these barbarians will be the end of me. Unless some beast devours me first!" *I'm no kind of hunter. And I could never be a herder, not like–*

The voice interrupted. *IF ANYONE WERE TO SPILL YOUR BLOOD, THAT SOUL'S SUFFERING WOULD BE FAR MORE TERRIBLE. FOR OTHERS' SAKE AND YOURS, I WILL WARN THEM.* A bed of stone lay under every word.

Len was baffled. *What is he going on about?* If the voice meant to reassure him, the effort fell short. Worse, the firebloom rivers began to inundate the first line of softly glowing foothills. The flowers melted into a nauseating wave of viscous red that rose over the hillscape. *It's too real to be a dream.* He was about to be drowned, and no soul could protect him from the torrents gushing toward him.

The woman continued to stare–sightless, unmoving, and of no use. All Len could think to do was shut his eyes and wait for the end.

Naught happened. When Len lifted his lids, the bloody wash of fireblooms and the otherworldly mist were gone. He looked confusion at the woman. *Or whatever sort of being she is.* Swirls of grey and green had returned to her eyes. Their gazes locked.

Yet something remained amiss. The more his fear ebbed, the more Len felt a disconcerting tickle across his brow. *When did that start?* He found he could move his limbs freely again and raised his hand to scratch the itch.

At this, the woman held up her own hand, palm toward him. Len guessed her meaning and lowered his; hers stayed. "'Tis for your own good," she sang in one ominous exhalation. To this she added, "Not to say you deserve as much."

Without further warning, the itch on his head flared. It swelled into a searing pain that made his earlier injury resemble a bug bite. *This is no waking dream. Am I afire, too? Is that my "good," what's best for me–to die?* Mayhap it would be better to perish, but he felt inclined to differ.

Uncertain what was happening, Len tried to surrender to the blinding torment. He wanted to scream but was unable to make any noise other than a throaty kind of gasp. Tears flowed afresh. He dropped to his knees.

Echoes of pain reverberated through the whole of his body for so long, it was some time afore he realized he'd been spared. Clear sight came back to him sluggishly. Close at hand, his digging blade lay in a clump of grass. That was where he left it. His focus settled on the ground before him.

When he reached up to feel his forehead, the touch stung. *But it's bearable.* His fingertips traced smooth, tender new ridges of flesh. Two slanting lines crossed his forehead. Each started over an eye, near his hairline, and crossed the other line above his nose afore ending at the opposite eyebrow.

"Leave this place we must," the woman interjected. She was altogether too solemn and calm for Len's uneasy soul. "You heard him." Shifting sideways, she gestured east, toward the wastelands.

We? Mayhap he looked as dumbfounded as he felt, for she deigned to clarify. "You are exiled, but my company have you, as a gift." A hint of begrudgment crept into her musical speech. "For your deliverance. Egwae am I called, and alive shall I keep you."

But why?

"Wonder, must you, the reason," she said, almost like she'd heard his question, "but I do not know. Suffice it to say, a role have you, some part or purpose that lies ahead. So obey, son of Ghrem. Come along."

Len didn't comprehend all she'd said, but he understood the last well enough. He staggered to his feet. *Don't reckon I have much choice.* He'd finished his downward trek, and east seemed as good a direction as any. *And I'll be less lonesome than afore. For the better?* He couldn't rightly say.

Chapter Five:
Wrought of Stone

Len reckoned he might as well have been on his lonesome. Egwae had said more to him in the first moments of their meeting than on any one occasion in all the seven-days since. As he trudged through sandy soil a dozen paces to her right, he recounted to himself the sources of his discontent.

These wastes. The parched air. The punishing heat. The scarcity of green and growing things. The sun blistering my flesh, excepting my mark. The mark–this disfigurement.

He wearied of the endless wandering. He regretted that he couldn't feel his feet anymore and that he could feel the ache in his legs with every step. He wished he could be rid of his goat-hair cloak, but he'd need it when he convinced the Wright to ease this curse off him. In the meantime, he felt smothered, even with it tied about his waist instead of hanging off his shoulders.

I hate the demon who led me this way. Egwae was likely right that heading south was the best way to avoid other folk and the trouble they brought. *And the trouble me and the demon would bring them.*

Less trouble meant he'd avoid mistakes–the kind that would keep the Wright from lifting the curse.

He loathed the curse most of all. *The one who laid it on me, too.* The Wright's words taunted him with the soil and the growing things now beyond his reach.

No mistakes. That was the only way to be rid of the curse, the mark, and the demon who came with both.

"How much farther you reckon we'll go this direction?" he asked Egwae. *I'm not sure I'll ever get the scratch out of my throat. Livyat take this dryness!*

After leaving eastward out of the valley, they'd turned due south. From there, they'd hugged the edge of the lesser Fangs. Keeping close to these bleak, worn-looking ridges gave Len the meager comfort that they wouldn't lose themselves in the wastes. He didn't know if a demon could lose herself. Then again, he wasn't certain she'd save him from dying of hunger and thirst the way she was bent on protecting him from every other hazard. *Anyhow, I don't favor the notion of having naught to look at but these sorry excuses for mountains the rest of my days.*

Egwae hadn't hastened to answer him. She never did. "Farther," she said at last.

Len quashed his frustration as best he could. "As you say, demon." He'd discovered quick how much that word rankled her. Egwae bristled, though she kept her long, gliding stride.

Len shifted subjects. "So, how does an unseen spirit get to being a dem– get to having a body earthly folk can see?"

He'd tried this sort of question afore and received naught in reply. This time, after several paces of silence, she responded. "Scions of the Wright are given many parts to play. A mundane form do these roles sometimes require."

Len mulled this over a spell. "Has he ever afore given you this sort of part?"

She didn't answer. *Still, she's more talkative than her wont. Might as well ask her something I truly want to know.*

"Is it possible for a body to get to the sky-realm? To the heaven-realm, I mean." That was what the demon called the Wright's domain. *It's what my folk call it, too.*

Len didn't expect a reply, yet she gave it within three paces. "Not for a soul that wasn't born there."

He supposed she was telling him true. *Demons can't lie, can they?* But the truth of it made little difference to him. *I need only be allowed back to the shade of the greater Fangs, where the soil's fit for growing. Mayhap as far as the hollow one day. Wright willing.*

The second of the sparsely vegetated foothills they approached had a mass of rock atop the waste side. When they drew closer, Len saw the protuberance wasn't a natural part of the hillside; it was a structure. *A dwelling. A cluster of them.* The round, thatch-topped stone buildings nestled comfortably among shrubby trees and patchy brush. *The smallest of them could swallow up our cottage.*

"Barbarians dwell this far out?" he exclaimed. "Why didn't you say as much, demon?" Len was at once fascinated at the spectacle and poised to flee. *But where to?* His mark was all a-tingle.

"All the earthly realm over do human-folk run amok," Egwae said drily. She didn't cast her eyes his way, but instead surveyed the stone structures, boulders, and brush.

"Then how in– how am I to keep from mishap? I can't make amends with the Wright if folk come to harm on my account." He felt the shame of those words at once. A chill rippled through the ridges of flesh on his brow.

The demon barked an awkward laugh. "You think you are the one to make things right, son of Ghrem?" she scoffed. She didn't take her wary eyes off the hillside. "Even death would be insufficient." Now she looked to him directly. "If some soul aims to harm you," she lilted, "no more innocent than you are they. But instructed am I to avoid unnecessary unpleasantness."

Len supposed the demon was trustable, as far as her priorities went. He couldn't see anyone moving around the dwellings. *Where are they?*

"As it happens," Egwae continued, "your cause for concern at present ought not to be human-folk."

What is she going on about?

A pair of tawny, long-toothed prowlers emerged from some hidden cleft in the base of the hill nearest Len and Egwae. Their vine-like tails swung to and fro as they stalked toward the two-legged beings.

"Look lively!" Len cried. "They'll close thirty paces afore I can run ten." *And they'll put two holes in me the Wright himself couldn't mend.*

Egwae sniffed lightly, as if to dismiss his panic. Yet she produced her fiery blade just the same. Grateful though he was to see it, Len shuddered.

One prowler leapt, and the other followed a split instant after. They were brawny as bears, but with fangs to make Livyat jealous. Len rushed to put Egwae betwixt him and the beasts.

Two leaps in, with only one more needed to close the gap, both critters halted in their tracks. Their heads snapped to the southeast, into the wastes. Almost as one beast, they sprang to motion again, leaping wide of Len and Egwae afore racing back toward the hill. The prowlers didn't stop there, either, but bounded upslope and disappeared over the crest.

It wasn't the demon that scared them off, like I reckon she scared the jackal that morning. But something ferocious enough to frighten prowlers... Egwae might have had a similar notion, as she kept her blade alight and pivoted in the direction the prowlers had looked.

They didn't have to wait long. *Is that a tree on the move?* Slow but steady, the grey tree became a grey hillock. *It's a critter.* As soon as it was near enough that the sun's glare didn't obscure Len's vision, he got a good look at the gargantuan beast lumbering in from the wastes. *The biggest critter I've ever seen.*

"Do not move," Egwae directed him. "Safer is it to hold your ground until it passes. Else it is liable to crush you accidentally." It seemed sound advice. Len stayed put and watched.

The critter crossed some forty paces in front of them, shuffling toward the nearest hill, where the prowlers had disappeared. Each of its trunk-like legs was as big as a man. With its tree-like neck, it was about thrice Len's height in all. Its sunbaked grey skin was wrinkly and hairless, so far as Len could tell. Compared to its massive overall proportions, its wriggly tail and twitchy ears were almost absurd. A beaked snout completed the downright oddity of the beast.

He'd listened, more or less, to his father and brother describing all manner of critters over the years. *They talked about tooth-nosed critters and tree-noses and tree-necks. Horses and hump-backs–I've seen those for myself now. But this one seems like all of those grafted together. The Wright has a sense of humor after all.*

Len hadn't the slightest what the proper name for such a beast was, if ever it had one. Naming critters couldn't be any harder than naming plants. *At a distance, it looks to be wrought of stone, like most everything hereabouts. Stone-beast.*

It stopped at the base of the hill to munch on scrub. While chewing a leisurely mouthful, it arced its long neck to and fro. Its black eyes swept over Len and Egwae without concern. *What kind of being or beast would dare trouble it?*

Len sat in the dust for a respite while he watched the critter eat its fill. At last, it turned and began moving south. *The selfsame way we're headed.* He clambered to his feet.

"Wait here will we until it has gone ahead a ways," Egwae said curtly. "In a small herd do these creatures most often travel. Ill-tempered or infirm may it be."

"Human-folk usually move in herds, too, but I don't," he retorted. *It's a wanderer, like me. Or a big, naked sheep.* A passing thought of Sceg and his bighorns brought him a pang of woe. It also gave him a sudden notion.

"I'm going to try something, demon. Only, it won't work if you insist on helping me after your usual way." He hesitated afore adding, "You'll have to trust me."

Egwae snorted. *But she didn't object.*

The first thing to do was follow the critter till it stopped somewhere. *For a drink, hopefully.* There was no activity or further sign of barbarian presence as they passed the hill with the stone structures. Len and Egwae trailed the stone-beast at a hundred paces. They walked in its three-toed tracks, afore wind and dust could erase them–Len on the right and the demon on the left, with only silence betwixt them. *As usual.* It seemed Egwae's earlier verbosity hadn't been a sign of more conversation to come.

The sun moved a good ways across the Wright's blue dome as they followed the grey giant. *Has it been here afore? Does it have a notion where it's headed, or will it know when it sees it?*

Sun-dazed weariness was setting in when a smudge on the horizon became an oasis. The first signs were the telltale treetops overlooking the watering hole: short branches, spread like the fingers of a hand, bore broad, feathery leaves. The beast waddled over to one of the palm trees and tugged off one of the lower-hanging fronds. After swallowing its snack, it arced its neck down to lap the water.

Len knelt at water's edge and drank several greedy handfuls himself afore filling his water pouches. He kept watch all the while to ensure the beast wasn't fixing to leave. *A critter that big in a country like this ought to take its time here.* He looked to Egwae, too, to make sure she was staying put. She glared back at him, motionless, from just outside the circle of palms. *Good enough.*

He approached the stone-beast from the far side of the watering hole so it could see him coming. At twenty paces, it retracted its serpentine tongue and tilted its head up to look at him level. Len continued forward, cautious-like.

The beast didn't go back to drinking; it stared at him till he got within ten paces. Then it raised its neck abruptly, stamped so as to shake the ground, and bellowed. Len re-trod his steps fast as could be, till he felt he was at a comfortable distance. The beast kept stamping and belting out its grating roar till Len stopped moving. Then it dipped its head to the water and resumed slaking its thirst.

Egwae hadn't budged. *She's uncommon patient today. Let's try again.*

This time, he took a more roundabout path to the beast. From everything he'd ever learnt about critters from his father and brother, it was imprudent to approach a dangerous one from behind. *I reckon I'm less than prudent.* Still, he kept a respectful distance from its legs. He went to the palm the beast had tasted earlier, which leaned so its top partly shaded the beast's back. He shimmied up the tree, ignoring as best he could the way the bark scraped and chafed his bare legs and arms. But the roughness gave him easy purchase for a rapid climb.

As he reached the palm's leafy pinnacle, he saw Egwae had moved closer to observe him with arms folded. *Does she walk, or just disappear from one place and reappear in another when I'm not looking?* He was grateful for the leeway she was giving him, whatever her reasoning. *Time to take full advantage.*

He pushed himself off the trunk and let go. *Wright almighty!* The moment he landed on the beast's back, it loosed a horrendous bellow. Len grabbed hold of the biggest fleshy wrinkles he could reach. In his grip, the critter's hide felt like grey leather.

The stone-beast stomped all four legs. It wiggled its hindquarters and shook its whole hulking body side to side. For good measure, it slammed against the tree several times. That knocked Len's right hand loose, but he held fast with his left.

Any moment, he expected Egwae to appear with sword blazing. *Except she's being careful. Because if she wounds it, it's liable to crush me.*

When none of its exertions served to throw Len off, the beast reared its prodigious bulk onto its hind legs. Len's mind went through every oath he knew and started inventing new ones. *But thank the Wright its hide is so dry. Else I'd have slid off from the sweat of my hands.* He felt he was clinging to the beast by a twig.

Len lost any notion of how long this continued. After a while, it occurred to him the sun had sunk close to the horizon. He ceased his silent cursing and pleading and simply hung on for his life.

Is the beast tiring? He thought it must be his imagining at first. But sure enough, its tossing and lurching grew more sluggish. Its bellows became less frequent.

Finally, sides heaving, the stone-beast stooped for a drink. Relief overtook Len like a deluge. He chortled hoarsely and then stopped himself. *It's tolerating me, but I oughtn't press my advantage too far yet.* He crawled up closer to the beast's bony shoulders. Grabbing hold of the massive folds of grey flesh, he pulled himself to a seating position.

Egwae stood beneath the next tree over and said naught; her expression was equally unrevealing. He grinned in triumph. “I needed another soul to talk to.”

She just stared, tight-lipped, until he gave up and focused on the thrill of sitting so high off ground. *Next best thing to being back in the Fangs.* Now he could roam more freely and range more widely. *Further into the waste, where folk don’t build and settle.*

Better yet, Len had a new companion. He patted its hide lightly. *One as ugly as I am. Who doesn’t know aught about a curse or a mark.* Circumstances were looking brighter. He relaxed his posture and watched the sun set from atop the stone-beast’s back.

Chapter Six: Reckoning

From his seat behind the stone-beast's elongated neck, Len looked over the endless sprawl of dunes. His throat was parched; his stomach ached from emptiness. Though he sat upon his goat-hair cloak, the incessant jostle of the beast on the move had rubbed his rear and thighs raw. The only hurts that sufficed to distract him from the soreness in his legs and hindparts were his chapped cheeks, irritated eyes, and bone-dry lips. Sandy grime filled every nook and crevice of his body, from the nails on his toes to his unruly beard to his eyeballs.

He pulled his palm-frond head wrap down over his ears. If this hat he'd woven to keep the desert sun off his scalp also happened to hide the mark on his forehead from the rest of the earthly realm, all the better. Try as he might, he couldn't forget the mark entirely. *Not with a demon slogging through the wastes alongside me.* Egwae's unrelenting presence served to remind him night and day off all the things he most wanted to forget. *I reckon that's why I hate her so. But no more than she despises me.*

The demon seemed determined to traverse the whole desert on her own two feet. Not once had she shown a hint of fatigue. Off to his right, just near enough to converse without shouting, Egwae strode resolutely across the sand-smothered earth. If she had a better notion than Len where in the wastes they were, and she likely did, she wasn't sharing. *So far east, we're liable to walk straight into the rising sun on the morrow.* But otherwise, he needed the stone-beast to reach the next watering hole afore dusk. There wasn't enough water left in his last pouch to keep a mouse alive for a seven-day.

Yet this was the only way. *The only way to keep clear of other folk. The only way to placate the Wright. I suppose he finds my circumstances entertaining. He's situated comfortable-like in his realm of clouds and stars, pondering what other curses and troubles he might devise for me.*

Surely the sky-lord was a fickle and sadistic son of a jackal. "But there's naught he can take from me worse than he's already done," he said under his breath. The stone-beast pricked its ears. If the boulderous critter had aught to add to Len's lament, its complaints weren't forthcoming.

His otherworldly companion hadn't reciprocated his attempts at conversation, either, these last few months. Whenever the demon broke her silence every half a day or so, Len found himself wishing she'd kept her peace.

"Rest yourself longer at the next oasis, son of Ghrem," Egwae called up to him. "You will longer endure these wastes if you tend yourself properly."

Suspicion flared. The demon seldom spared him a glance, let alone a care, unless it furthered her aim of keeping him breathing. But he sensed his demise would be more an inconvenience or disappointment than aught else to her.

"If the air weren't already so accursed hot," Len replied, "I reckon your concern would warm my heart, warden." His speech was as deliberate and unhurried as his mount's gait, to keep from catching in his dust-coated throat. "Warden" displeased her, but less than "demon." Not that he minded antagonizing Egwae. *But she truly is my warden, same as Father minding all the Wright's critters. Besides, it's more satisfactory to be a burr that snags in the hair than on the foot. Less of a hindrance in the moment, yet altogether more bothersome.*

"You know I'll linger nowhere the desert-folk may frequent," he continued. "I'm not as sociable as you are." He injected that final remark with a considerable dose of venom. Egwae wouldn't leave him to his own devices, and he couldn't escape or overcome her. Only his words availed him. They let him vent some small part of the pent-up fluster in his soul. *Of which I've had no lack since that morning the mountains bled fireblooms. What she did to Young Beard...* She'd done it on his account. And yes, he loathed her for it.

He couldn't make out Egwae's expression clearly in the late afternoon glare. Mayhap his verbal barb had no discernible effect. Even so, he allowed himself to think he'd stung her somewhere, beneath that cloak of dispassion she wore so tight.

The stone-beast tossed its grey-skinned head and snorted in what might have been amusement. "Leastways somebody here takes my meaning," Len groused. He patted the base of its tree-like neck.

Aches and pains aside, he was grateful for the beast in sundry ways. Afoot, he could never match the distance those ponderous, thick legs covered in a day's time. It had a keen sense of where the watering holes lay and, usually, as much interest as Len in getting to the nearest one straightaway. It could carry ample, or dwindling, food and water stores without difficulty. Best of all, the critter's sheer mass made for a sturdy bulwark against dust storms and other desert perils. *Like prowlers.*

Len preferred greener sorts of life, scarce though they were in this nether region of the world. *But I reckon I've grown a fondness for this great mound of a critter.* The tireless grey giant was the nearest thing he had to a friend.

Egwae, on the other hand, was the oddest sort of ally. *We'd be foes instead, if we had our druthers.* For a certainty, Len wanted to stay alive, and the demon was under some compulsion to keep him from harm. Her occasional suggestion to adjust course this way or that, without elaboration, had proven useful. He'd only ignored it once. And *I'd rather not spend another two days turning my beast from a she-beast's trail.*

Yet, survival wasn't enough. There was no point drawing breath if he couldn't return someday to the verdant land of the living. *So I'll convince the Wright to humor my wishes. Though he was the instigator of all this, with his cruel disfavor toward me, I'll keep his demon from harming anyone else on my behalf. Mayhap if I can sort out his intentions for me, the purpose Egwae spoke of, he'll end my exile.* Len would figure out what the Wright expected, and in somewise, he'd get it done. He would sidle his way into the sky-lord's good graces.

Failing that, I'll stir up the demon hordes of Livyat herself. Whatever it takes to get myself back to the land of rivers, rain, and decent soil.

"Your error, son of Ghrem," Egwae said, "is that you allow others to make your choices for you."

An irritable mood took Len over. He glared at her, but she kept her nose pointed forward as she traipsed along. "How do you reckon, warden?" He leaned heavy with contempt on that last word.

"Other souls kindle anger quickly in your heart," she answered, matter of fact, "so that the way your ire blows, to and fro, determines the course you follow."

Afore Len could offer a retort, Egwae added, "And fear rules you when anger does not. Hide from other folk do you, as if this will protect you. But in a story do you live, son of Ghrem, and wrought for a part were you." She searched for a word. "For a role in that story. Only two choices have you, in the end: do what you were made to do, or else be destroyed."

Disdain broke into the rhythmic lilt of her admonitions. "I should not have to tell the son of Ghrem and Lae that pointless is it to hide, and impossible to start over. To attempt either is as good as dying."

This final declaration cut so cold, it took Len aback. After a fleeting pause, he blurted, "What do you mean by that–you shouldn't have to tell me?" As soon as he uttered the question, he regretted the way it left him sounding ignorant and flailing. In consternation, he snatched the last water pouch from a fold in his repurposed cloak. A hot-tempered swig drained it dry.

Worse yet, Egwae didn't answer. *So be it. I should've learnt by now to mind my tongue.* The rest of the afternoon passed in sullen silence, save for the plodding steps of the stone-beast across the dunes and the occasional huff as it blew dust out its narrow nostrils.

Embarrassment compounded Len's want of replenishing. Thirst muddled his wits so he couldn't rightly ponder the things the demon had said. *She can talk all she wants of rest and tending myself, but she knows naught of such things. I reckon she's never partook of either sustenance or sleep.* But of parts and stories and purposes, she might know more. Her rarefied speech made for a goodly amount to digest. *After I've eaten and drunk my fill.*

So it was that the quiet, and the lazy sun nearing the end of its downward arc behind Egwae, brought an oasis into their line of sight. At first, Len could scarcely make out a dark, hazy smudge on the horizon. As the pale blue sky turned to orange and pink, the sharp-edged fingers of giant palm trees bloomed in his vision. *Wardens of the watering hole.* Sand drifts and clumped undergrowth betwixt trees completed a low natural barrier around the oasis.

The foreboding Len felt, as he supposed what unpleasantness might lurk by the water, was faint beside his pangs of thirst and hunger. Relief lay in wait for him, more certain than danger, and the anticipation lightened his soul. "Well done, beast–almost there!" So dry were his insides, the exclamation set him to coughing. His words of praise and exhortation had negligible effect. The stone-beast kept on at the same steady pace.

They were close enough to make out individual trees and bushes when dust clouds to the west, betwixt Egwae and the sunset, cut short Len's exuberance. He smacked the side of the stone-beast's neck. "Stop, you fool critter!" When that didn't work, he kicked down at its shoulders. With an annoyed series of snorts, the critter came to a halt. The stone-beast swiveled its neck and head toward Len to give him a pointed look with one black eye.

Egwae had stopped, too. She stared at the voluminous column of dust, which moved toward the oasis at an astonishing pace. *What's the likelihood a sandstorm would head straight for a watering hole? It's cutting too narrow a swathe, anyway.* Lan poised on the edge of his perch. Together with the demon and the stone-beast, he watched the clouds approach without comment.

If aught comes our way, I'll hide beneath the critter. Or flee afoot if need be. Only curiosity, and mayhap a lingering wound from Egwae's remark about fear, stayed him from leaping to the ground already. He felt a rising yearn to run east, into the endless oblivion of the wastes, as fast as his legs would take him. *Something's sorely amiss.*

Then the indistinct shouts of human-folk wafted his way. *Barbarians.* Len prodded the stone-beast urgently with his knees and feet. "Turn about! Quick now, or I'll leave you here!" Though its ears twitched, the beast found him as unpersuasive as ever. Its leathery hide rippled as it shrugged off his efforts. Unwilling to wait any longer, Len swung both legs to the right. He lifted his rear just enough to tug the cloak from under himself.

Just afore he dismounted, the cause of the dust clouds became visible. *Dromedaries. A dozen, mayhap, and all in a hurry.* At this distance, size was hard to gauge, but these stampeding hump-backs were clearly of the greater variety. *Twice my height, then, give or take.* They didn't measure up to the stone-beast in stature, but there were a fair few of them. And critters running scared were often unpredictable. *Like human-folk.*

Smaller silhouettes bobbed along the forward slope of each dromedary's hairy hump. From afar, Len had seen desert-folk riding hump-backs, but never in a rush like this. *Doesn't matter what they're about. It's past time to leave.* A night without water–or food to speak of, shelter, or transport–was preferable to a run-in with these barbarians. He pulled the cloak over his shoulders and launched himself from the stone-beast. The sandy earth swallowed his feet to the ankles as he landed.

"Stay," Egwae said levelly, declining as usual to turn her head his way. "Naught to fear from anyone does the son of Ghrem have in this place."

Len startled himself by barking an exasperated laugh, devoid of levity. "You know less than you think, warden." He hastened to give the stone-beast's forelegs more leeway. "Mayhap it's what those folk have to fear from you and me."

Inhuman sounds mixed with the vaguely human cries on the wind. *Are those snarls?* The stone-beast shuffled where it stood, a small mountain doing an anxious dance. With a twist in his gut, Len squinted at the cloud of dromedaries in the fast-failing light. They couldn't be much more than a hundred paces away.

Now he could see what he hadn't previously. Amid the billowing dust the hoofed hump-backs kicked up, a pack of loping jackals snapped at their flanks. Far larger than their mountain-climbing cousins, these desert jackals were fully half the height of their prey. *As tall as I am.* The beasts had less bear or wolf about them, and more fox.

These barbarians weren't thirsty. They were chasing their best hope of refuge, slim though it might be. The pair of souls, sometimes three, who straddled each dromedary were clinging for their lives, either to their mount's neck or to each other. *There are women-folk, too, and young ones.* Satchels bounced, and garments or tent skins fluttered behind the beasts' humps.

Len couldn't look away. He had come to a standstill, even as the barbarians and pursuing predators approached rapidly. They'd pass within a stone's throw, if not spitting distance, if their course didn't alter. In his peripheral view, the demon likewise held her ground. *By all reason, I ought to be long gone.* Duly spooked now, his stone-beast might feel tractable enough to carry him off in haste.

Yet he knew too well what it was to be in a dire spot, desperate, with no other soul to call on. *Wright knows, help doesn't always look the way you expect. Or turn out the way you want. But it's better than naught.*

"Help," Len croaked afore he comprehended his mouth was moving. *Livyat take me, I can't believe I want to inflict her aid on anyone else.* He forced resolve into his next words. "Help them."

"No." Egwae's voice was chill, more than her wont. *I wouldn't be surprised if she perceived all along that the jackals were there, hunting and harrying those folk.* "No concern of ours is their plight," she declared, just as flat and cold.

That settles it. Len knew what to do. *Well, I reckon I might.*

He started walking toward the oasis. After a few paces, he ran. Quick as could be, ignoring Egwae's reprimands and all his inner protests, Len rushed at the oncoming mess of beasts and barbarians.

For a longish moment, he could see himself from above as if he were a bird, weightless and aloft on a breath of wind. From the dusky sky, his self below looked all kinds of witless. *A fool ignoring the certain truth that other folk mean naught but trouble. They for him and he for them.* If he allowed himself another think, sense might knock him upside the head. It made him queasy–the vanishing space betwixt him and that flurry of hooves, claws, and dust in the gathering gloom. But the mere notion of turning about left him even sicklier.

Then he felt fully returned to his body. There was no time left to change his mind. Twenty paces away and closing, the lead dromedaries snorted, bellowed, and pounded the sand like rolls of thunder. The jackals gnashed their teeth and loosed bloodcurdling yowls betwixt vicious snaps and swipes at the hump-backs' legs.

Len's legs stopped churning as if of their own accord. The storm of terror and imminent violence buffeted his sensibilities so that he wanted to wilt in place. *Stand fast. For once, don't turn tail.* He let the tempest wash over him as he sheltered inside himself, like he might've sought cover under a rock. In that hiding place within, he found just enough presence of mind to act.

Len waved his arms, wild-like. He whooped, hollered, and leapt in the air. Though the dromedaries were too distraught to notice his antics, the nearest jackal peeled off in his direction. Several of its packmates followed. *They think me easier prey.* The first dog would reach him in a few bounds. *I've made a mistake. Leastways it's my last.*

He wasn't sure how Egwae appeared so quick betwixt him and the jackals. In three smooth steps, she produced her flaming blade and settled into a protective stance. *She does the simplest sorts of things in such a swift and flowing way. Like mountain runoff.*

Yet any hint of this liquid elegance disappeared as she laid into the swarming critters. Egwae wasn't water anymore, or a willow tree, but the wielder of lightning. Her fire-blade struck the jackals down with sudden, brutal thrusts and a jagged series of cuts. In the demon's hands, the weapon somehow seemed both precise and erratic. It was as if every stroke bit canine flesh by sheer accident.

The first jackal lost all its legs, fore and hind in succession. With a strike from high overhead, Egwae clove the second dog in twain from its nose halfway to its tail. Afore it hit the ground, she had disemboweled the third beast with a long thrust, which lit its hide aflame, and a cruel downward cut. A fourth critter fell in a dead heap without so much as a whimper when the unnatural blade severed its throat in passing. Blood sprayed, and red stains spread across the sand in the faltering sunlight. But not a speck touched Egwae or her pristine tunic. Len's face felt like stone as he watched the carnage unfold.

Soon eager howls and hungry yips had degenerated into confused, angry yelps. The only jackals left alive slunk off, into the shadowy dunes, leaving Len and his warden behind with the carcasses. Not a single dromedary or barbarian numbered among the bodies. At the edge of the oasis, hump-backs and their desert-folk riders slipped betwixt the palms.

Egwae rounded on Len. Ominous clouds filled her eyes of grey and green, and fury strained her countenance. He had maneuvered her into aiding the barbarians. *And she knows it.*

Len had more pressing concerns than the fact he'd riled the ruddy-haired demon. A third of the dromedaries wheeled about, rather than disappear into the palms with the rest of the herd. They wasted no time bearing down on him. Len had just saved these folk, but he looked unlikely to draw three breaths afore they trampled him into dust. *Only, the demon will never let them get that far. Which means I've got two breaths and a half to save them again.*

Afore he could make any move, a guttural, barbarous shout rang out. The dromedary in front skidded to a stop. It tossed its head this way and that in agitation. The other three critters halted, too, but paced restlessly.

All of the riders on these four hump-backs were men-folk, two to a mount. In age they varied, from a seven-day past youth to as old as Len's father. To a man, they looked proud and prickly as elm leaves, sun-tough as succulents, and solid-wrought as acorns. Their bright green eyes nearly glowed against their deep brown skin. Aside from the youngest fellow, they had thick black beards cropped short, straight as a blade, just below the neck. On their heads, they wore wide-brimmed hats of woven reed. They'd wrapped their feet cleverly in hide, up past their ankles. Snug waist-length tunics of dromedary hair hung open from neck to navel. A loose, leafy skirt hid each man's lap to his knees. *Desert-folk are a strange and splendid sort of barbarian.* And they made him feel positively naked in his britches and cloak.

The foremost rider of the lead hump-back, a round-faced man who was neither the youngest nor the eldest of the lot, held the knotted ends of a hide belt that was looped about his critter's head and betwixt its jaws. *That's how they halt their mounts so sudden. By tugging the ends of the belt.*

The barbarian leaned over the side of his dromedary's neck and shouted a throaty, lilting string of unintelligible phrases in Len's direction. They might have been commands or abuse, but either way, the words felt like a heap of fury. Len saw the man's widened eyes and recognized the precarious edge to his tone. Even the hump-back seemed terror-crazed in its snorting and stamping. *They want me gone, for certain sure.*

A discomfiting bramble of indignation and commiseration sprouted in Len. On a whim, he spread his arms wide and called up to the panicky green-eyed rider. "I'll not harm you," he declared. The desert-dweller kept talking over him, but Len continued. "If you'll just stay put, I'll be off! Leave me be!" Now the barbarian trailed off and stared, uncomprehending. *I reckon I should show him my meaning.* Len took a couple of slow, exaggerated steps backward.

Having ceased his tirade altogether, the barbarian offered a tentative nod and inquisitive-sounding reply. *He's guessed I intend to depart.* Len's heart thudded away, yet he allowed himself a slow breath and dared a hopeful glimmer.

With a few jerks on the hide belt, the barbarian maneuvered his dromedary into a sideways stance so the hump-back's flank turned toward Len. The round-faced man sat straight and used his hand to trace two diagonal lines in the air—one crossing the other, in front of his forehead. Len's gut tightened. *Serpents take the demon and this confounded, misfortunate mark!* Then the man spoke, harsh but shy of shouting. He pointed somewhere past Len, who didn't need to look to know he indicated Egwae.

It's not as if I expected thanks for saving these strangers. Nonetheless, it stung to be turned away once more, under a specter of death. *Faced with a hideously scarred wanderer, a woman who wreaks slaughter with unnatural fire, and a stone-beast half again the size of a greater hump-back, I'd want us gone, too.*

He yearned to make the barbarian truly understand. Instead, he kept backing up. More than thirst or hunger or aught else, he needed to be gone from this place. The desert-folk, rightfully afeared of what they didn't know, seemed inclined to give him his druthers. *On that account, leastways.*

Len heard the snarl afore he saw the jackal emerge from the shadows of the palms. "Look out!" he shouted as the lone beast lunged for the rearmost dromedary. A cacophony of bestial grunts and screeches followed, shivered through with the cries of men. All four hump-backs stampeded Len's way. Aghast, he let his arms drop limp to his sides. "No," he protested to the wind in resigned disbelief.

The demon and her fiery blade were there before him, so close he could've reached out and brushed her tunic. The dromedaries died with the last dim afterthought of the sun. Egwae severed their legs so that the enormous critters crashed into each other and then into the sand. Barbarians shouted in alarm as they fell from their mounts, afore being crushed beneath the beasts' humps or hooves.

In the pale light of the waxing silvery crescent above, Egwae was a shimmery shower of dusty earth and blood. The jackal pounced on a hump-back it had crippled. An eye-blink later, Egwae's blade carved clear through the dromedary's thickly muscled neck on course to lop the head off the jackal.

"Stop it!" Len screamed, over and over with such stridence that his throat burned and his voice broke. "Mother of Serpents take you and your confounded Wright!" For a few fleeting heartbeats, the chaos drowned him out, even to his own ears. So overwhelming was the acrid stench in the air all around, his stomach heaved. Yet he forced himself to stand his ground. He willed himself to watch the devastation he'd brought about.

Soon the noise subsided, excepting the shrieks and wails of those desert-folk who had found refuge in the oasis only to see their kin perish. *So I might carry on my wretched existence.*

When Egwae finished her deadly dance, she extinguished her weapon and strode toward him, gliding spirit-like past the bodies of beasts and barbarians. He stared dully at her moon-graced shape.

"You should've let me die, warden," Len accosted her with a savage bite.

Though he couldn't spy her expression, he thought her reply reeked of satisfaction. *Livyat's lair, but we do share a special kind of hate.* "Clear is the purpose my lord assigned me," Egwae said, "and it requires you to live." Her tone hinted this was an unwelcome necessity.

But she considers the bloodletting fair recompense. Because I dared force her to save helpless folk from hungry jackals. Such scant good that accomplished. Mayhap, instead of avoiding folk, he ought to try the opposite. That notion prompted another. *Instead of persuading the Wright to let me work the soil again, I could find others to grow things on my behalf. In which case, I needn't wait on him to lift any curse...*

"Well, I suppose I know what I'm about, then," Len said with a detached sort of calm at odds with the frightful tremors in his heart. "My purpose, you might say." *The demon is fond of that word, purpose. It might finally be growing on me.*

Egwae didn't offer any comment. Like as not, she didn't know what to make of his utterance. *That's just as well.* Len's soul was awash in an unfamiliar kind of exhilaration.

First things first, he'd take the demon's earlier advice after all, to rest and replenish himself here. *It's shuddersome to imagine sleeping anywhere near those piteous desert-folk. Mayhap they'll choose to flee by moon instead of huddling under the palms.* He let resolve harden his heart. *Either way, I'll do what I must.*

His grey-skinned companion would surely find its bed at the oasis, too. *Come dawn, I'll collect the belts these barbarians used to guide their critters. I'll fashion them into one fit for the stone-beast. I reckon I could wrap my mind around the task after an evening's respite.* In the meantime, he would gather up plenty of foodstuffs and fill his water pouches. They'd set out westward on the morrow, Len and his somewise trusty mount.

With the demon in our wake. Time for my warden to prove of real use to me. They had more wandering to do together, but with a purpose. Soon enough, it would be time to wander no longer. When they departed the wastes at last, there would be a reckoning for the grievous things Len had suffered. *Mayhap I've uncovered my part in the Wright's story. And he and the demon might wish I hadn't.*

Chapter Seven:
The Sand-Rabbit

I've got an uncanny feeling we're being followed. "But who would trouble to follow our sorry selves is beyond me," Len told the stone-beast.

The beast snorted but didn't break stride. *This critter won't stop till it reaches water or nightfall. Unless today is the day it starts minding the guide.* After a few seven-days, the stone-beast no longer fussed at the belt of dromedary hide in its mouth. Yet it didn't pay attention to the directions Len gave with the guide-belt, either. *I'm less liable to fall off in a dust-dazed stupor when I grip the ends, leastways.*

"It must be some kind of desert critter. We haven't seen any sign of human-folk since that tent village yesterday, and there wasn't a soul thereabouts. And now we're in the middle of the wastes. So why do I feel we've got eyes on us?" *I suppose a one-sided conversation with a roving lump of leather is preferable to a two-sided conversation with myself.*

Len cast a languid look over the dunes to either side. He could scarcely see aught past the midday glare. *Son of a snake, this must be the hottest place in the earthly realm.* Swelter and light filled the dry air so full, there wasn't space for a drop of moisture. He imagined the momentary relief the next desert wind would bring. Anything was cool by comparison with the dead heat that otherwise ruled here. *That's what my existence has come to. Waiting for the breeze to blow my way.*

He hoped the sense of being watched wasn't some unseen spirit, like the eyes on him as he descended the Fangs. *I'd ask the demon about that, if I didn't loathe her so much. I would ask her if some servant of Livyat is tailing us now. Even then, she might not say. So I'll just keep asking myself. I mean, the beast.*

"A sand-rabbit."

"What's that, warden?"

Egwae waited a good several paces afore she repeated herself. "A sand-rabbit follows us," she said, in the deliberate manner Len's mother had spoken to him as a child.

Surely I'm not comprehending her meaning. Of course, he wasn't about to admit as much.

"Since we left the village behind," she explained with a weary edge to her tone.

She means human-folk? "But there wasn't a soul in sight!"

"There was one," she countered.

Of course she wouldn't tell me aught of significance till the morrow after.

What kind of folk would sneak through the wastes after two strangers and a stone-beast? A hunter? *It doesn't matter. I'm not hiding from folk anymore. Though they seem to be hiding from me at present.*

He shook his head. *But I don't need any distraction, either. Not from demons or spirits or folk of any kind. I've got a purpose to sort out.*

To that end, he needed to find the rest of the dromedary-riding barbarians. The survivors of the debacle with the jackals had made themselves scarce afore dawn-break. He'd tried following their trail. Only, they knew the wastes better, and their dromedaries were faster than the stone-beast. Sand and wind made quick work of tracks.

Is that who's following us now? Mayhap one of them warned off the villagers and that's why the place was empty. There were too many unknowns. Len tried to muster patience and came up short.

Exasperated, he told the stone-beast, "This so-called sand-rabbit must be using the dunes for cover." *Because there isn't so much as a rock or shrub to hide behind in these parts.* "Let's climb the dune to the south and see if we can't flush out this mysterious fellow." *Distraction or no, I reckon I'm a mite curious.*

The stone-beast sighed. Sometimes Len could swear it comprehended more than it let on.

He tugged left on the guide-belt. The stone-beast shuddered and tossed its head indignantly, but Len only tugged harder. *It gets the gist, leastways.* So as not to squander time, he threw in a few kicks to the shoulder and a smack on the side of the neck. After a whining bray, the critter obliged his prodding. It veered grudgingly south, toward the nearby dune. The demon kept abreast of Len and his mount without comment. *Never a step closer or farther from her ward.*

In irritable silence, the three of them traversed the windward slope. Len's held a long breath with quickened pulse when the stone-beast climbed unnecessarily close to the treacherous eastern slipface. *It knows better. This is its vengeance for my heavy-handed persuasion.* The critter didn't look like much of a climber, but it was sure of foot and took them to the crest without incident.

From the top of the dune, Len turned and searched for any sign of life or movement. *Naught but dust.*

"She's still there," Egwae sang afore he could comment to the contrary. *She? Wright, anything but another she-demon.* Fluster swelled in Len's chest.

Ahead lay a ravine-scarred plain, which offered a few flecks of pale green. Beyond, more dune ridges and valleys stretched all the way to cloudless blue. *We're so far lost, not even the Fangs can find us.*

The stone-beast didn't linger but immediately began its descent down the far slope. Now it avoided the slipface by a wide margin. *The ornery critter's made its point, I reckon.* On reaching the foot of the dune, it started across the sun-scorched plain at once. But when it came to a gully, a crack as wide as Len was tall and twice as deep, it hesitated. Egwae casually lifted her face heavenward while she waited at the edge of the chasm. *As if she sees all the way into the Wright's realm. Mayhap she does.*

"Don't stop now, you great hornless aurochs!" Len berated the stone-beast. That earned him a wholly unperturbed backward stare from a black bestial eye.

Of all the stubborn snakebit critters, I had to cross paths with this one. Len gave his mount a firm yet polite nudge with his knees. "Keep moving. If you please." He swallowed a scowl.

The stone-beast snorted and returned its attention forward. It extended a tentative foreleg and pondered a moment. *That's it.* The beast stretched itself over the gully, which left Len in a precarious spot till it achieved its footing on the other side. Its other feet followed in quick succession and carried the rest of the critter, with Len, across the divide. Egwae leapt over without effort. *As easy as taking a step. Like she's floating on a current.*

On a sudden notion, he looked over his shoulder. A slight figure in a tunic slipped down the leeward side of the dune and scurried their way. *The demon spoke true. Whoever it is, she couldn't be all that threatening. But she doesn't know who or what she's scuttling after. Does she?* They needed to press on.

Surer of itself now, the stone-beast crossed the next gully, and the one after, without trepidation or fuss. *That ought to dissuade her.* As if in answer, the figure bounded up to the first chasm and took a running leap. Her dark hair streamed behind her as she flew over the gap.

By the ever-living Fangs! Enough of this. Len yanked on the guide-belt with both hands, left and right and then back with all his strength. The hide strip cut into the tender flesh of the stone-beast's mouth. With an angrified roar, it reared its head. Len ignored its distress as best he could and kept pulling the belt every which way. He hugged the base of the beast's neck with his legs and held the guide-belt tight as the critter stomped, thrashed, and worked its jaws. *Surely this'll scare her off.*

In its throes, the beast got turned about so that Len wound up facing the dune, back the way they'd come. And there, not a dozen paces distant, stood the woman.

She was a short, green-eyed wisp of a thing clad in dromedary hide. *Those are the eyes I felt.* Strands of tightly curled hair hung in a face the hue of late-autumn acorn. She brought to mind the shrubby oaks that grew up the sides of the Fangs.

Instead of retreating from the stone-beast's tantrum, the barbarian woman approached. When she came within five paces, she stopped, gave a shrill cry, and barked three times. The beast recoiled and froze in place. *Not what I expected, either.*

The barbarian glanced at the other woman present, who hovered close by the stone-beast. Egwae placed her hands on her hips. *The demon's not pleased, but when is she ever? And she's not fixing to interfere.*

Without warning, the critter swooped its neck low to stare levelly at the newcomer. Len barely kept his balance. *Would someone here start acting normal-like?*

He thought at first the barbarian was of an age with his mother. *But other than those crinkles, she has a youthful aspect. The wastes add years.* Her jaw was set. *Ornery as a shrub-oak, too.*

Yet her expression belied something else. *Fear of some kind. Fright? Awe?* For the first time, their eyes met. *It's not the critter she's leery of. It's me.* He touched his head wrap to ensure he'd pulled it as low as could be on his brow.

The woman's attention reverted to the stone-beast when it cleared its nostrils pointedly. A softly guttural stream of words poured out of her. The beast settled to the ground as if transfixed, tucking its legs carefully, as she continued the purring speech. *Some rabbit.* Len had assumed she was human-folk, but with such power over critters, she could be a demon. *Or mayhap she simply has Father and Sceg's gift.* He swallowed hard.

"Kaelii," the woman said. She looked from him to Egwae and back again. Perplexed, Len shifted his eyes betwixt the barbarian and the inscrutable, ruddy-haired demon.

"Her name speaks she," Egwae said as if relieving his ignorance caused her injury. She responded to the desert-folk woman in what

Len took to be the same barbarian tongue. He caught a feline-sounding "Egwae" amid the breathy intonations. The woman, Kaelii, inclined her head respectfully.

"Len," he blurted. When she looked up, he said more slowly, "I'm Len," and pointed to himself. Kaelii nodded, but she appeared no less trepidatious.

"Kaelii," she said again, with a tap on her own chest. "Eg-wae," she said, indicating the demon. She jabbed a finger at him in turn. "Len." Then she said his name once more, but followed it with a sound like a prowler coughing up fur.

"The name she gives the creature," Egwae explained, "is Len the Large." The faintest glint of wry humor peeked through the demon's indifference.

"Big Len?" Len sputtered in disbelief. *We've only just met, and her first inclination is to call the critter Big Len?*

Kaelii, nonplussed at his reaction, said something else while walking her fingers through the air. Then she indicated Len and the others.

No need to translate. "She's wanting to come along. With us. Why in– Why would she want to do aught like that?"

Egwae and Kaelii had a brief exchange while Len hopped down from the stone-beast. He worked the bow out of his legs and tried to stretch the soreness out of his travel-weary backside.

"With a query of her own does she reply," the demon said. "'Why does Len want to walk the wastes with a giant and a spirit?'"

Len scowled. *If only she had an inkling.* The company he already kept was nuisance enough. *And Egwae won't protect another soul like she does me. I don't reckon a sand-rabbit will long survive this close to demon fire.*

Both Kaelii and Egwae were glaring at him. The desert-folk woman spat defiant words, which Egwae relayed as soon as Kaelii took a breath. "Stories has she heard already, of the wanderer who rides a giant and brings destruction." *The demon can say this without batting an eye?*

"Her folk listen to the wind," Egwae continued, "and it tells them many things." The demon sniffed. "Or so she says."

Len felt suffocated under the others' stares, and the sun's tendrils burned his flesh. *Wright almighty, but I'd escape all this in a heartbeat. And I can't escape any of it.*

"Son of Ghrem, mayhap consider allowing her to accompany you," Egwae added. "More good than harm may it accomplish."

Len's sluggish mind did its utmost to ponder the demon's counsel. *Curse the cloud that spawned her. In all the earthly realm, I reckoned she'd be the last to want more human-folk about.*

Egwae was a truthsome being, but surely her advice was a trick or a trap in somewise. *For me, or for the desert woman.*

He met Kaelii's bright green stare. *A sand-rabbit won't survive what we're about, but a shrub-oak might.* "I must be sun-addled," he mumbled.

He shuffled over to her across the hot sand so only a pace and a half remained betwixt them.

"Well met, Kaelii. I reckon Big Len can carry two souls as easy as one. And you'll be a better traveling mate than this pair, sure as dust."

Egwae had resumed her usual, impassive demeanor. When she translated, Kaelii raised her eyebrows. The barbarian woman replied, and the demon answered. Then Kaelii burst into a guffaw and slapped her knee. "Mate," she mimicked afore another wave of laughter took her over.

Len's cheeks warmed in a way that had naught to do with the wastes. He hadn't a notion what was so funny. But he got the distinct impression he'd erred again.

Chapter Eight:
Lord of the Wastes

Len gestured to a pair of the grunting hump-backs roaming the barbarian camp. "Remind me, what do your folk call those?" he asked Kaelii in a subdued tone. Side by side, they followed their reluctant escorts. The two straight-backed men used hunting spears as walking sticks and moved to the same silent rhythm.

Kaelii raised her eyebrows and furrowed her forehead. "What you call?" she asked.

Her voice is like leaves rustling. She's learning my language a sight faster than I'm learning hers. "Dromedaries. It means they run fast when they see fit to. Or we– I call them hump-backs." He waited in vain for Egwae to translate. "Put it in her speech for me, warden," he prompted.

From behind them, the demon replied, "Most certainly will I not."

There was no sense pressing her. Len pointed at one of the giant critters that loitered near their path through the tent village. It had its nose shoved to the ground as it scoured the sandy soil for aught remotely edible. *I wish I hadn't had to leave Big Len behind for this.* "Dromedary," he told Kaelii.

She sent her curls bouncing wild-like with a quick, vigorous toss of her head. “Camel,” she declared.

The men they passed wore open vests and leafy skirts; the women wore longer skirts or tunics. Every one of them paused his or her activities to give the strangers a green-eyed glower of loathing and fear from under a broad-brimmed hat. *Not all of us. Me.* Len was sure of it. Even the children stopped frolicking at their approach and stared or else skulked away, toward the tents in the center of the camp.

A barbarian with the beginnings of a beard ran up close. The boy spat at Kaelii and screamed at Len, who moved betwixt his companion and the youth. Taken aback, Kaelii watched the latter skedaddle.

She shouldn’t be here. But shrubby oaks were obstinate things.

One of the escorts shook his spear at the brash youth’s back and shouted words that sounded like reprimand. *But his heart isn’t in it. Our guides hate us, too. Can’t say I blame them.*

Len spared Egwae a look over his shoulder. *No fire-blade.* But the demon’s countenance said there were limits to what she’d tolerate from these desert-folk.

“Mate, folk no like,” said Kaelii uneasily.

“You’re telling me,” he muttered. *The stories got here afore we did.*

They hastened to catch up with their escorts, who’d continued ahead. The glares continued unabated. But without further altercation, they arrived at the circle of irregular domed tents, some three dozen all told, in the middle of the village. The spear-bearers wound their way around the first few tents on their way to the largest of the camel-hide domes. They flanked the open door-flaps and looked expectantly at Len.

"I'll be all right in there," he suggested to Egwae. "You might give these folk the jitters. And Kaelii catches my meaning well enough to translate." *It's true enough.*

"That alters naught," the demon said.

Kaelii offered him a forced smile. "No worry, mate." *She's aiming to convince herself as much as reassure me.*

Len grimaced and ducked inside.

The inside of the tent smelled like sweat. Light flooded through a gap in the roof and filtered through the hide walls. The space was full of twenty-odd men and women arrayed on a single circle around an empty fire pit. Some of the barbarians sat cross-legged on mats while others propped against piles of beast skins with legs splayed.

Most of these desert-folk looked his parents' age or older, with at least a few wrinkles and streaks of grey in their dark hair. *Where are Father and Mother now? Do they think of me?* He hoped they didn't.

Not a soul spoke. All their eyes were fixed on him. And displeasure verging on fury consumed every face.

Excepting one. Unlike the others, he sat on a low stool. *He's a short fellow.* The man was stocky and solemn-faced. Whether this barbarian was Len's age or ten years older, Len couldn't say. *But he's the head of this lot.*

Kaelii and Egwae flanked him now. He moved to the center of the tent and heard their footsteps follow. It was so quiet, Len heard the breeze over the hole in the roof. Somewhere outside, a camel snorted.

The leader spoke gruffly. "He asks, 'Who are you?'" Egwae said.

Len thought for a breath. "I'm Len.' That didn't seem sufficient. 'Len–the wanderer. Son of Ghrem and Lae. My companions are Egwae the Warden and Kaelii the–"

"Kaelii of the Wind Hunters," Kaelii volunteered. *Wind Hunters?*

Egwae gave Len a fleeting frown afore she passed his words along. *Or what she wills of them.* Len resolved to teach Kaelii more of his speech, and to learn more of hers, starting on the morrow.

Murmurs rippled around the circle of seated folk. The solemn-faced man on the stool didn't flinch.

A wizened old woman, by appearance the eldest soul in the tent, made a short utterance. Then another said something, and another. *Their names.* Len stayed his eyes on the leader while listening distractedly to the barbarians' introductions. *He's the one I'll have to persuade.*

Finally, only the man on the stool remained. "Krækw," he said, direct to Len. After a calculated pause and two additional strings of words, he resumed his straight-faced stare.

"The elders of the Camel Lords are they," Egwae offered in summary. "And Kræwk is their chief. He wishes to know why you trouble his folk."

"I don't wish trouble on any soul," Len replied. "But I bring their folk a proposal." *Here goes naught.* "Join me. Follow me out of the wastes to a green country where water flows in many streams."

Egwae's flaming blade was nowhere in sight, yet Len wondered if the demon's eyes might skewer him where he stood. *She must have gathered my intent afore now. Or suspected, leastways.* He almost thought she wouldn't relay his answer to the others assembled. When she did, the Camel Lords erupted in fearful indignation.

Kræwk hushed them with a bark and a wave of his hand. Impatience and ire had broken across his stern demeanor, which remained fixed on Len.

A woman with more than a middling amount of grey in her hair rose, all a-tremble, to her leather-wrapped feet. As soon as the chief gestured to her, she pointed an accusatory finger, first at Egwae and then at Len. The woman startled Len with a rageful onslaught of words, which degenerated into grievous wails. At length, she sank to her knees and sobbed quietly.

Len realized he'd been neglecting to breathe. *The oasis. The jackals.* The demon, meanwhile, seemed to have endured all this unaffected. *Do spirits have souls the same as we do, or merely the semblance?*

When Len looked over to Kaelii, her expression was sorely perturbed. "Who did she lose?" he murmured.

If Kaelii didn't comprehend his every word, she guessed his meaning readily. "Daughter mate die," she whispered back. Revulsion colored her inflections. *Egwae killed the husband of that woman's daughter. Because of me.*

Len discerned an unwonted weight in Kaelii's expression. *No mischief or levity. No reassurance. She's having a second think. I'll be on my lonesome with the demon afore the day is finished.*

Kaelii gave his arm a staying pat, which left him momentarily afluster, and stepped betwixt him and Kræwk. She bowed at the neck before the chief and spoke in a conciliatory manner. Kræwk replied tersely, but the creases in his brow lessened.

They continued back and forth for a spell. *Serpent's fangs, I hope she knows what she's about.* She surely seemed to. It was odd to hear beseeching and mollifying tones woven into Kaelii's usual firmity. The chief looked less put out, though by no means pleased.

Something Kaelii said elicited a nod from Kræwk. "What did you say to him?" Len asked.

Kaelii launched into a long-winded reply in her native speech, which Egwae began rendering into Len's tongue afore the desert-folk woman had finished talking. "She tells him, 'My friend the wanderer intends no offense. He regrets the presumption of his request and the blood that was spilt. It was a terrible accident. Yes, he looks and speaks like a beast. But beasts are powerful. The fire-spirit who accompanies him is powerful, too.'"

And I was afeared Egwae would take liberties in translation. Presumption, indeed! She'd given him the benefit of the doubt, leastways.

As if it were an afterthought, the demon added, "The sand-rabbit asks, as well, what the Camel Lords desire from you in exchange for their aid in your quest."

The sand-rabbit says a lot. "What was Kræwk's answer?"

"'Green land and running water are well and good,' the chief says, 'but the dead have little use for such gifts. Dangers abound under the sun and the blue. We will consider helping the wanderer if he grants us protection from spirits and strangers who would destroy us.'"

Spirits and strangers aside from Egwae and me, he means.

Kaelii interjected. "I say, Len yes. Kræwk want Len say now."

He wants to hear it from me. Fair enough. Every face in the tent seemed cast toward him. *I'd do my utmost to keep them from harm. There's no accounting for the demon. But they don't need to know that.* Egwae looked fire-blades at him. Kræwk's pondering expression pierced him through. *Or about any curse. I'll just have to be strong enough to protect them.*

Len's gut twinged the moment afore he nodded gravely to Kræwk. "You have my oath. I'll protect you." *She's my warden. I'll learn to be theirs.*

The chief didn't wait for a translation. He shifted from his stool to his knees on the mat in front of him. Then he lifted a finger and traced the sign of Len's crosswise mark on his brow.

It was all Len could do to suppress a shudder. He averted his gaze and caught the demon examining Kaelii. For her part, the desert-folk woman studied Len. She favored him with a smile. It didn't quite banish the leeriness from her eyes.

Chapter Nine:
Children of Dust

Sweaty trails streaked the weary, sun-wrinkled face of the chief who knelt before Len. The man's green eyes shifted, uncertain, from Len to Egwae and back again as he mumbled a stream of guttural phrases with hardly a pause.

Beside Len, the warden looked down at the barbarian with seeming disinterest but translated for him, anyway. "Of the man who bears the sign has he heard," Egwae drawled, "as well as what befalls those who stand in his path. The Children of the Sunset Dunes, his clan-folk call themselves, and follow where you lead will they."

She finds it amusing, this soul declaring his fealty. "You must be right pleased, warden, by the way events are playing out," Len remarked lightly. For a rarity, Egwae seemed puzzled at his meaning and looked him a question.

Len let slip a grin. "I reckon you were getting tired of being the only one to follow me about."

Egwae bristled at the notion that she was in any wise subject to him. But she held her tongue. Len's smile cracked his dust-caked face so wide it hurt.

The kneeling chieftain drew both their attention by taking a swig of water from the pouch slung over his shoulder and making a harsh, hocking sound. Then the barbarian scooped up a heaping handful of sand in one palm, spat into it, and proceeded to smear two muddy streaks across his own brow.

Well, that's a new thing. A lump formed in Len's throat, his smile vanished, and a fleeting chill shivered his spine. The lines were an imitation, clear as the pale blue sky, of the mark burned onto Len's forehead. Egwae scowled outright.

But Len, perturbed though he was, stepped forward. He reached out to lay a hand on the barbarian's bare, black-haired head. *Seems like the thing to do.* Wide-eyed, the man looked up at him, more anxious now than afore. *He's afeared I'll harm him.* Unnerved, Len withdrew his hand and retreated a hasty half-pace.

"I'm called Len," he told the barbarian, pointing to himself. With the other hand, he gestured for the fellow to stand. The chief obliged, cautious-like. "What your name?" Len asked in desert speech. He made an inviting gesture and tried his best to convey reassurance.

"Hrogg," the barbarian said, with a hand pressed to his chest where his tunic opened in front.

"I'm glad to have you, Hrogg," Len replied with a curt nod. Then he added, "Tell your folk to break their fast and water their beasts, if they haven't. You'll be riding with the Children of Dust today."

Egwae snorted afore she relayed the words to Hrogg, but Len didn't pay her mind. *I nearly named them Children of Wrath. I wonder how she'd have liked that? It was her notion, with her talk about my ire making my choices for me. I reckon she had the right of it.* But all told, Children of Dust seemed more apt a name for his company of wandering souls.

With a casual sweep of the arm, Len welcomed Hrogg, and the cluster of desert-folk behind him, to join the throngs congregated on the surrounding dunes. The several dozen newcomers shuffled past. Men-folk in their brimmed hats led camels of the smaller sort and gave him surreptitious, guarded looks. Most of the women-folk, herding excitable young ones, wore hooded tunics and expressions of concerned wonderment.

That makes eight clans all told. Camel Lords, Sand Folk, and Wind Hunters. Sons of the Prowler, Children of the Palm, and Waetii's Folk. Scions of the Dawn. Now, Children of the Sunset Dunes–there's a mouthful.

On the dunes, Len's folk milled about, striking the final few tents and packing the last of their belongings. None of these souls he'd encountered in the wastes looked quite like him. The desert-folk were shorter, with deeper complexions, thicker black hair, and eyes of green or darkest brown. Their garb varied from the scantiest-clad Wind Hunters to Waetii's band, swathed in camel hair from head to toe, and the gamut betwixt. They all tied their satchels, rolled hides, and bundled tent poles to the backs of their camels.

The Camel Lords' mounts loomed over their lesser cousins. Every dromedary in sight had a drooping hump. *We need to find water early today.* Kræwk and his family had already loaded up their camel and were leading his folk down the long windward slope of the nearest dune.

Serpent's spawn, but it's a hard thing to get accustomed to, having so many folk around all the time. Added to that, he was responsible for all these souls and their critters. Len hadn't considered that side of things when he'd chosen this path. *It's naught I can avoid now.* This was the way.

That way was closing, gradually, on its ultimate destination. "Sunset Dunes" was another reminder that they'd returned to the western marches of the wandering wastes. A little farther west, a little farther north, and Len might again lay eyes on the river-lands, hill country, and mountain peaks from which the Wright had banished him. *I'm not ready yet–but soon.* What would happen then, exactly, remained to be seen. *I reckon it's up to the Wright. And Egwae. And all these folk with me.*

Len turned around and tilted his head sharp to look the stone-beast in its scrutinizing eyes. "What?" he grumped. "It'll work." Mayhap his plans lay counter to the Wright's confounded curse. But the spiteful lord of the heaven-realm wanted him preserved, for some reason or other, which meant Egwae wouldn't stop him when the time came. *Will she?*

Big Len peered at him past little folds of grey skin and his beak-like muzzle. The critter dipped his long neck and exhaled warm, dusty air out of his nose slits–into Len's face. Len coughed and wrinkled his nose in dismay.

"Ask pardon, mate," sang a voice from above. A fluttersome laugh followed. "Big Len wants no hurt." Atop the stone-beast sat Kaelii, as natural as if she'd been born holding the critter's guide-belt. *Reins, she says.* A new palm-leaf kerchief held back her curls from her acorn-dark features. Today the shrub-oak was a desert rose, cheery and pleasant to look at. *Yet full of hidden mischief.* Len returned her a half-hearted glower.

"Where we a-riding today?" Kaelii prompted when he was slow to say aught.

Her speech may not be perfect. But at this rate, she'll soon speak my tongue better than me. I ought to practice hers more. "We'll let Big Len take us to water, first off. After that, it depends. How many clans lie betwixt us and the hills?" He pointed due west, toward the lesser Fangs he knew lay that way, beyond their sight.

Kaelii feigned annoyance. "You ask like we no talk this afore."

She's right, confound it. I asked her the same already this morn. There were so many details to keep track of nowadays. *Life is simpler when you're only responsible for your own self.* He missed that simplicity.

Len opened his mouth to defend himself, but Kaelii pressed on, her demeanor full serious. "Sand Folk say kin at big waterhole. No many tents. Two dawns." A pair of bony fingers made certain he understood. "Six and six dawns, Stone Pickers make stone tents at Fangs."

The stone dwellings. Len hadn't thought much about the hillside full of barbarian structures they'd seen the day Big Len crossed their path. Kaelii was giving him an unconvinced look. *Building in stone might seem a dubious effort to desert-folk. But when we're living beneath the Fangs, it'll be a different story.*

"Clans no big," Kaelii stressed, "but Waetii say seven and seven dawns north is big clan. Many tents. Bone Jackals."

Not the most hospitable-sounding folk. "You got Waetii to talk?" Len asked. So far, he'd not heard Waetii herself say more than two words at once, and she wouldn't speak to him direct. Kaelii waved a dismissive hand.

"We'll find the other Sand Folk," Len told her after another moment musing, "and the Stone Pickers, too." Kaelii furrowed her forehead skeptically. "There's a terrible lot of stone where I'm from," he reminded her. "Mayhap you'll want to live in a stone tent someday." Kaelii and Big Len sniffed at the same time. Len glanced betwixt them warily.

Egwae's knife-edged lilt cut in, as the warden crossed behind Len and called up to the woman on the stone-beast. "Ask him, desert daughter, when he plans to stop his meanderings about the dunes. Better yet, ask why he insists on picking up more things lost in the desert." *The demon's fluent in every tongue, seems like. I wish she'd say more I didn't understand.*

If Kaelii didn't grasp every word, she had the gist. "They call it wastes of wander, no for naught," she said with forced sweetness. Len couldn't altogether keep himself from smiling at the demon's grimace.

Ignoring Kaelii now, Egwae bored her grey-green eyes into Len. "Remind me, son of Ghrem," she inquired flatly, "does the sand-rabbit up there fit your schemes?"

"I'm sure she does," he lied to her. *And she was your notion.* The warden poured all her disdain and disregard for him into a silent, stone-faced stare. *I reckon if I could be back in the Fangs by my lonesome, I'd take the wolves and jackals and nightmares every day, over this she-demon.*

Big Len interrupted with a loud, lowing noise and stamped, eager to move out. A look up at Kaelii, adjusting her position high on the stone-beast's back, told Len she likewise wearied of the conversation. She noticed his attention and flashed him a cheeky grin.

"Neck hurt, no?" Kaelii said. "Head look up too much. Here now, mate." She rubbed Big Len betwixt the shoulders and clicked her tongue like a woodpecker. The stone-beast crouched low enough for Len to clamber up a leg to the critter's back. He took his usual seat behind Big Len's neck, in front of Kaelii. After handing him the reins, she reclined against two bundled food sacks. They'd secured the bedrolls, water pouches, and stores of dry food with fibrous cords cinched around the beast's girth.

Over his shoulder, Len said, "Thank you kindly." For no good reason, the words came out clumsy.

Kaelii didn't remark on his fumble. "No worry," she replied.

Len decided Big Len had the right of it. *Time to move out.* The day was well on its way to sweltering, though the sun wasn't long in its eastern ascent, so they needed to make the most of the morning. With a flick of the reins, and a scuff of his feet against the stone-beast's shoulders, Len gave the critter leave to get moving. They lurched forth and ambled along, slow enough for the desert-folk to finish their preparations and fall in line.

The caravan formed without any command from Len or Egwae. Some of the clan chiefs, and no few mothers of young ones, shouted exhortations at those who yet scurried about. Near every morn, for seven-days beyond count it seemed, they'd followed a similar rhythm, excepting the Sunset Dunes' arrival shortly after dawn-break. By now, Len's folk knew what to do.

Kræwk and half the Camel Lords cantered past Big Len on their way to the front of the column. The chief called a greeting too quick for Len to comprehend. The stern-faced fellow insisted on riding ahead. Even so, they'd learned to heed Big Len's instincts. *Because he won't heed theirs, sure as the sun goes down.*

Egwae might've been the most predictable in all their company. She walked alongside Big Len, even with the beast's shoulders and, so, immediately to Len's right. All the other folk kept clear of the tall, flame-haired woman. A few had glimpsed what horrors she was capable of effecting, and all the rest had heard stories aplenty.

Mostly, Len trained his sight on the horizon as they wound westward. Traveling with so many souls and their critters meant predators kept their distance. *All the better to think on where I'm headed than where I'm at.*

Pretty as the sun's rays might be, piercing the clear sky and glancing off the wind-carved dunes, the desert air remained dreadful dry. It would be hot enough at midday to wilt rock. *I'll never be able to grow a garden in this place. Or anywhere, if the Wright keeps his curse upon me.* Wistful pangs of powerful longing for the hollow and meadows throbbed deep within. *There's no hope here.*

That glum truth aside, Len would have felt his situation greatly improved by a proper hat of that wide-brimmed sort many desert-folk favored. *I'd even take my old hat about now.* If only he hadn't let Kaelii's smirks and needling get the best of him, he might have kept the leafy head wrap. '*Skinny sick palm tree,' she called me. My dusty rump!*

His present musings produced an unintended grumble from his throat. "What your trouble?" came a question from behind. Kaelii sounded earnest, but Len was in a wallowing mood. He answered with an ambiguous grunt.

Instead of letting up or giving him an earful, she said, "We give wind our trouble, mate. Wind scatters like sand." Then they lapsed into silence again, left to their respective ponderings and to the low rustles, murmurs, and bestial complaints from the caravan to their rear.

Truth, there was naught like the expanse of the desert to make a body aware of the delicate state of things. All critters perished sooner or later. *"They just get tired of living," Mother told us. "Men-folk and women-folk, too, after a while." She never said why, only that we'd all turn to dust someday.* And it never made much sense till he found himself stuck in the wastes. Living and breathing under the sun was an exhausting business. *Besides, it's the only way the demon will ever let me be. If I fade like a flower past bloom.*

Len took a long pull from his water pouch. *What's it like to be delivered up to the wind?* Critters in the Fangs made it look like falling asleep. He imagined emptying himself of troubles and watching the warm wind blow them away.

Over the course of the morning, he drained his water pouch and started on a second, his last. *It's a hot one.* The train of human-folk and critters trudging behind the stone-beast found the going especially difficult. They'd grown so unwontedly quiet as midday approached, Len couldn't help but turn every so often simply to ensure they'd not fallen by the wayside. Even Kaelii held her thoughts close. Whenever Len stole a glance, she either swayed with eyes shut or stared skyward and sipped from her water pouch. Only Egwae seemed unaffected, except for shortening her stride so she wouldn't outpace Big Len in his sluggish shambling. *We're moving slower today.*

Just as Len started to wonder if the stone-beast had lost his knack and led them astray, Kræwk and his folk approached a small oasis. It looked to be naught but a stand of stalwart palms guarding a modest watering hole, but neither the Camel Lords nor Big Len hesitated. The grey giant perked its ears and plodded over to the water, bypassing for the moment the tufts of pale grass and assorted succulents that adorned the sandy earth nearby. Egwae moved off, without comment.

Big Len began guzzling water like some kind of gargantuan tree root. Kaelii and Len shimmied down the stone-beast's forelimbs. Len stretched the knots from his legs and watched the camels, greater and lesser, flock to the waterside.

"No big water," Kaelii observed. "Beasts drink all gone." Len just nodded. *Thirsty as the critters are, they're liable to drain it dry.* Though hump-backs didn't need to drink or feed often by human reckoning, they sure could fill themselves fit to bust when they had the opportunity. *And they've been surviving off the rare patch of dune shrubs for some days now.*

Afore the press of barbarians and beasts around the watering hole could hem him in, or Kaelii started feeling more gregarious, Len took a cue from the warden: he walked off a ways, by his lonesome. Already the sun beat so merciless upon his head, he knew he'd have to scrounge a spare hat from somebody afore they departed this place. *Not that anybody in the caravan wouldn't go bareheaded for my sake, if I asked.* They were all too afeared of his unsightly mark and blade-wielding companion to deny him aught, but he wasn't about to take advantage. *Any more than I must, leastways.*

For now, Len surveyed the landscape. The high dune ridges they'd been following the past three days ran east to west. Ahead, though, they tapered off. Afore the afternoon was spent, their caravan would cross the north-south ridge visible on the far horizon. Beyond that, Len couldn't see, and he had only the vaguest picture in his mind. *When we camp tonight, I'll get Kaelii to ask Hrogg's folk and the Sand Folk what to expect.*

The sudden perception of movement in the middling distance snagged his attention. Len frowned and squinted. All he could see was an odd smudge, mayhap two hundred paces off. *Or is it more like one hundred?* He found the space betwixt him and the dark blur strangely difficult to gauge. *A mirage?* There was no discernible haze in the air to distort his vision.

The indistinct form seemed to quiver for several heartbeats. Then it stilled. Len blinked.

Without warning, the thing appeared fewer than a dozen paces off, though Len hadn't seen it move another twitch. *By all that draws breath–what is it?* This critter most certainly wasn't a mirage. It stood on two legs, likely a few hands taller than Len, but he could imagine no folk further from a man. With gnarled limbs and a featureless visage, apart from two exaggerated black eyes and slit-like suggestions of a nose, the apparition was like a shadow incarnate. It wore no clothes; its hue was pallid grey, unvaried other than its eye-pits.

Len's instinct was to recoil in startlement and raise an alarm. Instead, he found himself transfixed. If this being's eyes had irises or pupils, he couldn't see them, but he felt the intensity of its stare down to his bones.

What's a snakish spirit doing so far from the Fangs? Without a doubt, he was seeing the unseen. But there was naught here to interest Livyat in this desolate country. *Is there?*

Though this demon had no mouth, Len heard a sibilant voice in his ear. It was as if the being were the size of a squirrel and perched on his shoulder.

"The dust of the earth betrays you, son of Ghrem," the uncanny voice murmured. "We see the stains that mar your soul. Follow the way of wrath. There your redemption lies."

Despite the heat, ice pricked his veins.

"Mate!" called a more familiar voice behind him. "On two feet you sleep?" Len blinked again. Now the sinister spirit had vanished.

He turned to show Kaelii–and Egwae, several steps ahead of the desert-folk woman–that he wasn't dozing or daydreaming. He continued to scan their surroundings, too. *Is the demon gone for true? Mayhap it simply slipped under the surface of the seen. Either way, what does it want with me?*

When the women reached Len, Kaelii lifted her chin and studied him. Her green eyes glinted in the sun and gave Len somewhere new to focus. She placed one hand sternly on her hip. "You need water. And hat." Kaelii proffered him an exceptionally floppy, wide-brimmed hat he hadn't realized she clutched, nearly folded in half, in her other hand.

Distractable as he was, Len didn't accept the gift straightaway. She finally thrust it to his chest, and he took it from her. The hat was in somewise fashioned from soft camel hair and hide, not dried grasses or plant fibers. *Where'd she come by this?* It wasn't quite like aught he'd noticed any of the barbarians wearing. Len set it on his head and found instant relief for his sunbaked head. *Not bad.* He tugged on the brim.

"Thanks," he said. Kaelii grunted agreeably, but her eyes passed his by. *She seems distracted, too. What did she see?*

Egwae, by contrast, seemed tense, like she was one nudge shy of producing her fiery blade. Her gaze swept the dunes to the north while she spoke to Len. "Encounter something, did you, son of Ghrem?"

He didn't know how to explain what had transpired just afore their arrival. Instead of answering direct, he responded with his own query. "How far outside Livyat's lair can her servants range?"

Sure enough, Egwae looked straight at him now. *Without a hint of surprise.* Grey-green eyes shone with suspicion confirmed. "The Wright permits the chaos-spawn to roam wherever water flows and gathers across the earth," the warden said. Over Kaelii's head, Len looked at the dense crowd of human-folk and critters encircling the waterhole. *Or mayhap there's a hidden source, like the ones that feed the desert shrubs.*

"Yet their power wanes the farther they stray from the Mother of Serpents in her prison," Egwae continued. "In these lands, unlikely is it for her minions seen or heard to be. By an earthly realmer, leastways. Unless, that is, some other spirit or soul made the chaos-spawn an opening." Her eyes narrowed. "Someone who exercises power over the dry earth."

"Bad spirits here?" Kaelii interjected. He hadn't considered how much or little of this exchange Kaelii might be following. Her eyebrows knit in alarm. "We hurry quick from here."

Len ignored her and asked Egwae, "How might a body find these servants? If they aren't looking to be seen?"

Lightning flickered in Egwae's stormy eyes, and Len could've sworn that a humorless smile threatened the tight corners of her mouth. "Only as my duties require does my lord give me knowledge, son of Ghrem. But seek the chaos-spawn if you will. And discover for yourself." There was no mistaking the dare in her inflection.

Kaelii, disgruntled that they talked past her, had none of it. "You have no care. Say fool questions," she told Len. Concern poked through her accusatory tone. "Bad chief hunts for troubles." She looked exasperation at him, with a touch of expectation. At a loss, his mind flitting to and fro, Len returned a blank stare. Kaelii heaved a sigh and flung two flustered hands to the heaven-realm. She stomped off toward Big Len, who grazed on palms over the other critters' heads. Len felt suddenly loathsome. *I ought to have paid her more mind. I'll offer apology later.*

"This once do I warn you," Egwae told Len, as if the words were extracted with considerable pain, "Livyat ruined those who begat you, and I doubt not that it gratified her soulless self to see you tear your life asunder."

Len's blood ran cold from his chest to his fingers and toes, more so now than at the sight of the serpentine spirit. He fought to wrest his stomach back down from his throat. *I can't recall the last time she mentioned why I left home. What happened that day.* He didn't welcome the allusion. Belatedly, he absorbed the rest of what she'd said. *What does Livyat have to do with Father and Mother?*

"The Mother of Serpents–not I, and not the Wright–is your enemy, Ghrem-son," Egwae added. "So if you'd be the wiser, beware *actual* demons. Not me."

For an instant, her words' breathy weight buffeted the thick hedge of resentment in Len's soul. *Might be she has a care, after all. But she's still the one who marked me.* The moment passed; the hedge held.

"Egwae," he asked, "will you prevent me from doing the things I intend? Departing the wastes? Will the Wright keep me from going home?"

Thoughtful curiosity softened the warden's angular features. "Mayhap," she answered. "Together will we learn, I suppose." Discomfort stiffened her expression once more. She turned to go–and then paused, head tilted and eyes cast to her shoulder. "But disobedience is a burden that crushes. Only so much can you carry, son of Ghrem." With that, she walked away.

No matter her intent, Egwae's warnings left Len undeterred. Standing there alone, he felt newly emboldened. *Whatever burden comes with the path I'm on, I've got others now to help me bear load. I have my part, and the Children of Dust have theirs. We'll each of us be who we're wrought to be.*

Chapter Ten: Stones and Dust

Kræwk bounced along on his camel's back. "Mayhap we see this green country soon," he suggested.

From the front of the howdah, Len looked down at the Camel Lord chief. "Not yet," he said in desert speech. "North next. Then west to big hills and river-lands."

Kræwk grunted. "We talk to Stone Pickers first." He sounded unenthusiastic.

Behind Len, Kaelii added, "The wanderer comes from the stone teeth. There we find stones and trees as far as the eye sees. We need folk who build with earth and stone and wood." She'd begun speaking slower and clearer of late. *For my sake, I reckon.*

"As you say," the chief replied. He sounded dubious.

They'll see for themselves, none too soon. "I ride first now," Len said with all the authority he could muster. When Kræwk nodded grudging assent, Len continued. "We reach Stone Picker big village. You tell other Camel Lords, watch caravan. You and chiefs come with." The barbarous speech still felt strange in his mouth, but it got a bit easier every day. *Recalling the words I want is the trick.*

On the front slope of the camel's hump, Kræwk's young son broke free of his mother's grip and threw himself onto the critter's neck. The boy pointed excitedly. A small, dusty mountain loomed ahead. *The lesser Fangs. It's been a while.*

Kræwk spoke rapidly with his wife, who scooted forward to secure their son. *She's with child.* The chief turned his face up to Len once more and made a crosswise sign over his forehead. Len raised a hand in salute and practiced keeping his wince on the inside. With a bellowed command to the other Camel Lords, Kræwk fell back in the column. *Making the sign is for their sake, Kaelii says, not mine. It's my part to make all the fuss worthwhile.*

As if she discerned his thoughts, Len felt the encouraging pat of Kaelii's slender hand on his back. *Leastways she and Kræwk don't paint the mark on their flesh. Too many of them do.* Her reassuring gesture felt conciliatory–all the more so when she sat down beside him. She didn't say aught, but her choice to be so close was notable. It wasn't that she'd been unfriendly, exactly, since the day she gave him the hat. *More like she's been somewhere else.* Together they watched the Stone Picker settlement come into view.

The village on this mountain was larger than the one where Len and Egwae had found Big Len. Mayhap a dozen thatch-roofed structures were big enough to see from this distance. *And that's just the east slope.* The main building occupied the whole of the gently rounded summit.

"Look, mate," Kaelii said in his speech. "Little horn critters!"

Sure enough, dark dots turned steadily into knots of bovines spread across the mountain slope. The mountain was scarcely more than a foothill, compared to the greater Fangs. Yet the beasts stirred up yearnful feelings he hadn't expected.

"Aurochs," he told her. *If those are little, what's a big horn critter?*

When Kaelii didn't repeat the word, he glanced over. Her expression was somewhere far away.

"Wha–"

"Quiet!" she said. *She's scared.* "Hear the wind."

There was a westerly breeze coming off the lesser Fangs. "All I hear is the sound of beasts and folk shuffling through sand."

"Son of Ghrem!" Egwae's voice, sounding from below, sent a chill through him. *Wright, I forget she's there.* He peered over Big Len's left side into the warden's grey-green eyes. "To the south," she said.

The instant Len obliged, his mind emptied and dread swept in. A blurry, narrow band was just visible betwixt the edge of the desert and the blue dome above.

There aren't any hills over yonder. The band was growing thicker by the heartbeat. "Dust storm," he said with a calm he didn't feel.

"Merciful Wind-breather!" Kaelii exclaimed. A stream of prayer to the sky-lord issued from her lips. *Couldn't hurt.*

A cry arose behind them and echoed down the caravan. "Dust cloud!" Len snapped Big Len's reins and looked back at the caravan.

All eight clans–men- and women-folk, young ones, and critters–stretched halfway to the eastern horizon. *I can't protect them from this.* Desperate shouts filled the air, and unless Len imagined it, more dust than usual. The column dissolved before his eyes as every clan, family, and beast sought its own survival.

Big Len sensed the storm a-coming, or leastways picked up the urgency all around. After Len's initial prompt, the stone-beast gathered speed till he reached a full-fledged gallop. Len's body rattled to his bones, but he wrapped the reins around one arm and held his hat in place with his free hand. Kaelii clung fast to him and kept praying.

The cloud to the south had quickly become a rising wall of sand. On the mountainside ahead, Stone Pickers herded the aurochs into outlying buildings.

Try as Big Len might, the Camel Lords' beasts, and even some of the lesser dromedaries, soon overtook him. The last of the Stone Pickers and aurochses vanished into their dwellings just afore Kræwk's folk won the race to the mountain. They immediately set about ensconcing themselves in the boulders at the bottom of the slope.

Come on, boy. You'll make it. We have to make it. Len's heart thundered in his ears with every round of rumbling footfalls.

In the same moment Big Len finally skidded to a stop, the sun dimmed. *But it's only mid-afternoon.* The looming wall of sand was blocking out the daylight. Sustained gusts buffeted the howdah. When the stone-beast clambered into the rocks of his own accord, Kaelii hugged him tighter, and he leaned into her. Though dark curls fluttered in his face, that was preferable to the sting of wind-blown dust. Kaelii held herself rigid with fright.

Big Len wedged himself betwixt several sizable boulders and knelt of his own accord. *I wonder how many of these storms he's seen. Is he even nervous?*

"The coat!" Kaelii shouted over the whipping wind. "It will keep dust off."

"I'll get it! Wait a moment!" he yelled back, which sent sand spewing from his beard. *Where do I think she'd go?* The stone-beast was still settling himself when Len released Kaelii and his hat. He disentangled himself from the reins and snatched his cloak from inside the howdah while Kaelii grabbed water pouches and slung them across her chest. She pulled her palm kerchief over her mouth. Instead of putting the cloak on, Len held it aloft, over both their heads. Kaelii adhered herself to his side.

Egwae appeared next to the stone-beast's head. *Not a speck or a smudge on that tunic.* "A crevice is there, under the boulders near the beast's posterior. Shelter there." They didn't quibble with her. Len scrambled though the howdah and out the back. He turned to help Kaelii, but she pushed past him and hopped off Big Len's rump to the rock-strewn earth.

Egwae had made her way onto the beast's back just as quick. Such was the growing gloom that the warden's white tunic was all he could see clearly of her. "Make haste!" she commanded. Instead of finding her own cranny to cower in, she sat herself at the front of the howdah. *I don't reckon I've seen her sit afore.*

"No dawdle, mate!" Kaelii called. Len jumped after her. *The warden will see to herself.* Kaelii, scant more than a silhouette now, beckoned to him. A pace from Big Len's hindquarters, two of the boulders left a space big enough for the both of them. Sand flurries chased him into the crevice, where he tucked himself next to Kaelii. She nestled close as could be. Together they huddled under the cloak as he held it across the opening.

Utter darkness descended outside their makeshift refuge. An angry gust tried to tear the garment from him. Kaelii's hands brushed over his as she helped him hold their goat-hair shield in place.

Len's breaths came ragged. *It's not the dust. Not yet.* A crushing weight bore heavy on his soul. "I can't protect them. I promised. But I can't."

"Whole life they live in wastes. We know how survive little dust cloud." Kaelii's kerchief muffled her reply but didn't dampen her ferocity a lick.

The weight on him lifted just a bit. If he had to be in a tight spot like this, he was grateful for the distraction of company. *Her company, anyway. Bloody fangs, I could've been holed up here with the warden.* It was a shame he couldn't get a semblance of privacy from Egwae—and the chiefs, and everyone else—without all their lives hanging in the balance.

"Egwae is brave," Kaelii said in a tentative tone. "She watches you. Good mate."

A chortle set him to spluttering. *Not all the dust is keeping out.* "Sorry. She's my warden. Not my friend. She protects me because she must."

The howling wind assailed their hideaway. Even with Kaelii's help, holding up the cloak was noticeably more of an effort. *Sand is piling up.* He didn't fancy getting buried alive. *Not that I have much choice. One problem at a time.*

Kaelii cleared her throat roughly and coughed. "You want Stone Pickers build tent? Len's stone tent?"

"A house, you mean. I suppose I hadn't pondered much on it. Mayhap." *My own cottage of stone and earth, in the shade of the Fangs. There's a notion.*

When she didn't comment right away, he tried putting more of his thoughts to words. "It's part of my purpose. What I have to do. I want our folk to build things and grow things. Because I can't build and grow them my own self."

Silence persisted, save for the roar of the sandstorm. "I want stone house," Kaelii said at length. She was half-shouting to be heard. "In Len's fangs. There wind from sky talks loud."

"Louder than the wind out there?"

"No make fun," she protested.

"I'm not," he assured her. "I think I'd like a stone house. What more do you want when we get to the valley–the green country?"

"A child," she said at once. She continued in a more measured way. "A child make me happy. Make my mother and father happy, too. First time I make them happy."

"Your kin-folk seemed pleasant enough when we met."

Kaelii snorted and then coughed. "Try be their child."

"I was a child, too, back in the day."

"Len was boy in Fangs, yes. I meet your mother and father?"

Didn't see that coming. "They'd like you," he said.

"That no answer."

Sky-lord save me from this woman. The darkness had somehow turned darker. *Storm's not letting up.* The sand piling on the cloak posed an uncomfortable strain on his arms now. "Not sure they want to see me. In fact, I reckon they don't." The admission stung him deep.

"Kin are–many? Mess?"

"Complicated. And a mess besides. But in my family, I'm the messiest."

"Why you say that?"

Shame whelmed him over. He felt like telling her his story, the whole of it, but held back at the last instant. "I'm like them," he said finally, "yet different." The words spilled out betwixt sips of air. "I wanted to do things the way I saw fit. Sometimes, that was good. Sometimes bad." *Worse than you could imagine.* He was feeling more trapped in the space, of a sudden.

"I had my thing to do," Kaelii said. "My kin not know why." *She's having a harder time breathing, too.* "They no need know. But they kin. Like mates. No throw away."

The shame that swallowed Len up at her words contended with the sweetness of her voice. He concentrated on the feel of being squeezed in beside her.

"Len?"

"Yes?"

"Mayhap we make stone house in Fangs? Real mates, you and me?"

His cough was only partly the fault of the dust-clogged air. *Don't go lying to yourself, Len. You want the same as her.* But what he wanted and what he could have were separate matters. Something was sorely amiss inside him. He was broken like the Fangs and dry like the wastes.

"I'd like that, Kaelii." He'd given a truthsome reply, yet he remained a muddle inside.

They had to use their breath more sparingly now. The last of their conversation hung betwixt them while they waited for the chaos on the other side of the cloak to subside. *Wright, I hope you heard her praying afore.*

Len had allowed himself to slip into a kind of stupor when the wind slackened. He didn't trust his senses till a faint light bloomed at the edges of the cloak. *Storm's passed.* An indistinct voice was calling. Gradually, more light crept in, and the weight of the sand lessened.

Dust swirled around Kaelii's sand-streaked face. She smiled. Something bright and fierce crowded out the consternation in his soul. He smiled back.

At last he dared to push the cloak aside. Kaelii released her grip on it, too. "We good, mate," she croaked with a wide grin. "See, a little dust."

Egwae stood in the haze at the opening of the crevice. "Son of Ghrem," she said. *Is that a touch of relief I spy?* If so, it was gone too quick to be certain.

"Hello there, Egwae," he greeted her. Kaelii handed him a water pouch for the scratch in his throat. The warden arched an eyebrow. Her eyes flicked betwixt them.

"We go now," Kaelii broke in. "Time a-wasting."

So it is. More than I knew.

Chapter Eleven:
Lords of the Valley

Times beyond count, Len had dreamt what it would feel like to crest the final dusty ridge betwixt him and the rolling river-valley. Deep-rooted as his attachments ran to the northerly Fangs, his memory hadn't accounted for their sheer scale. *Even afore I met the warden, I whiled my days roaming the slopes, not gazing up from their feet.* From the high places, he couldn't appreciate the mountains' grandeur the way he could now.

Snow gleamed upon the loftiest summits as if they lit the pathway to the heaven-realm. *Mayhap they do, at that.* After so long wandering in the arid wastes, the existence of snow strained credulity. *How long since I last laid eyes on those peaks?* Somewhere along the way, months had turned to years. But seasons felt different in the desert.

The sight of trees and scent of flowing water in the distance had the stone-beast anxious to press on. *He's not the only one. At last, land that's alive and growing.* Wistfulness waxed in his soul at all the green. *I wonder if the beast has ever come across so much fodder and drink.* Len leaned forward and patted Big Len on the neck. "You'll like the low country." Such an enormous critter seemed better fitted for the woodlands than the dunes.

Anticipating that he'd find the valley cool after all his time in the wastes, Len wore his goat-hair cloak over his bare torso. *Just like the day I left.* Only, now he had his floppy hide hat to shield his eyes from the midday sun. He'd also traded his old plant-fiber britches for the trousers of soft dromedary hair Kræwk's folk gifted him. Begrudgingly, he'd adopted the desert-folk habit of wearing hide covers–*boots*–on their feet. After a lifetime going barefoot, he almost felt too comfortable. *Almost. Sand can get unseemly hot, after all.*

To his right, Kaelii whistled long and low. "You say true, mate," she called up to him from her camel's back. "Big Fangs are big." *Confound me if that critter she's procured isn't the scrawniest bull camel in the wastes.* He missed her company in the howdah. She seemed pleased as could be, sitting there atop Rabbit.

"They're even bigger up close," he told her. *Of course they are. What a fool, obvious remark.* Kaelii didn't reply, so rapt did she stare at the mountains ahead.

Egwae likewise refrained from comment. The warden stood betwixt Big Len and Rabbit and looked somewhere high in the Fangs. *Or above them?* Usually, she kept precisely abreast of Len and his mount. At present, she stood a few conspicuous paces behind the stone-beast's shoulder. *She'll force me to be first into the valley, if I'm so determined.* Well, he was.

Hundreds of desert-folk and their beasts had arrayed themselves on the bare hillside behind Len. The thirteen clan chiefs, most on camelback with their mates and young ones, were strung out to either side of Big Len and Rabbit. Kræwk had brought his family up close on Len's left. The Camel Lord chief kept a steady hand on his son, who looked set to leap from the great-camel and scale the Fangs himself if left to his devices. Kræwk's wife held their wee daughter, swathed in a fur blanket. All of them, down to the infant, bore the crosswise mark on their cheek.

Len didn't like it one bit. *Though I reckon I can learn to endure the sight.* The Children of Dust might follow him, yet they were a powerful stubborn lot. Nowadays, every soul Len saw seemed to have a marked forehead, or sometimes a face or arm. *There'll be no mistaking them for the valley-folk.*

The other chiefs were taking in the expansive view. South of the valley, the semiarid lesser Fangs lay in humble quiet. In front of Len's assembled folk, the river wound its way into the distant west like a shining blue serpent. The Fangs rose highest there and in the north. Two camels past Kræwk, normally jolly Dubrhos uttered a reverent oath. Silent awe had taken the rest over. *Except Morii.* On the far side of Kaelii and Rabbit, the tousle-haired Stone Picker foreman rode his bull aurochs alone. Morii stroked his scraggly beard thoughtfully. *He and I might be the only ones who've really seen the greater Fangs afore, excepting Egwae.*

Len breathed deep and savored the hint of moisture in the wind. He was almost home. *As close to home as I might ever get.* The soil might not yield him its fruits any longer, but only the Wright and the warden, or Livyat herself, could stop his folk from crossing the valley threshold. *And yielding them its bounty.*

A herd of aurochs grazing on the south bank of the river drew his attention. The bovines must be at least as tall as him, yet at this distance, they looked like long-horned beetles. On the north bank, hills and trees abounded. The earth was mostly flat and lush, with scattered woods and broad, wind-swept meadows. *And human-folk.*

Barbarians moved about the far bank like meandering ants. *I reckoned we'd meet them sooner or later. Sooner, looks like.* Since Len had left the valley, they'd settled the north side of the river in villages of pointed tents and earthen mounds.

This won't get any easier. "The day will escape us, if we gawk long enough." Kaelii nodded. It was time to find out whether all his plans and preparations would come to aught. "Warden," he said to Egwae below, "we're going to cross that river into the valley. Does the Wright have a mind to stop me?" *Are you, Egwae, going to stop me?* Heads turned; the nearest clan chiefs had heard his question. Kræwk, leastways, probably understood it.

Egwae didn't answer right away but tilted her chin skyward and closed her eyes. Len held an apprehensive breath. Finally, the warden brought her gaze down to the valley landscape and sighed. Her tone sounded disappointed when she said, "Permitted is it." Then, low for Len's ears, she added, "For now."

Len exhaled relief. *'For now' is good enough for today.* Like a fire had been lit beneath him, Len stood and secured the reins to their peg on the front of the howdah. He ensured they were taut, to cool the itch in Big Len's feet. Then he snuck through the howdah and out the back end, where he balanced himself over the stone-beast's hindquarters.

The mass of folk assembled on the barren slope looked at him expectantly. A wee one cried out till its mother placated it. Len cleared the dust from his throat.

"I was born up yonder," he began in desert speech. He gestured to the northern heights. "That is my home. I am the firstborn child of the firstborn lord of the stone teeth." *Though Father would laugh to hear himself named as such.* "And the teeth rule the valley." Nary a breeze stirred.

"You are my folk," Len continued, "so you, Children of Dust, are now chiefs of all from this hill to the sunset. Everything betwixt the big teeth and the little teeth is yours." He made a wide arc with his arm. The desert-folk met his declaration with astonishment and scattered whoops.

"Every clan takes its land," Len said, "for tents and beasts and food. You will learn to grow food from the ground." That prospect elicited fresh murmurs and exuberant cheers. His heart swelled. "I will teach you!"

Len tried imbuing his voice with added strength and solemnity. "Folk who live here now will fear you. They will run. Later, mayhap some join us. For now, no worry. Follow your chiefs."

The response to his final words was subdued. *That might not have been the best way to conclude.* What he'd said was said. He returned to squat at the front of the howdah and took up the reins once more. With a flick, he started Big Len forward. The stone-beast didn't need to be told twice. But a little way down the front of the ridge, afore the critter could pick up speed, Len pulled back and brought him around to face the chiefs at the crest. The stone-beast snorted its dissatisfaction. Kaelii had walked Rabbit downslope in Big Len's tracks, while Egwae lingered nearer the top.

Len called up to the chiefs in his own tongue. Exact meaning was of utmost importance now. "See that great bow in the river, in the shade of the tallest Fang?" He drew in the air to make clearer his intent as Kaelii translated. "Where the river bends out from the foothills and back again, afore winding its way to the center of the valley." Kaelii stumbled a bit over that part, so Len continued more slowly. "We'll cross inside the bow here, on its east side. The water won't be deep there, close to the wastes."

Once Kaelii caught up, he added, "As soon as we cross, spread out. Lead your clan, each of you, to claim a territory you'll then lord over." At this, Kræwk and several others voiced hearty assent.

"But see that barbarian village there in the cluster of hills, where the foot of the biggest Fang sticks out a bit?" He pointed. "That will belong to the Stone Pickers. You understand, Morii?" Hunched over his heavy-laden aurochs, the foreman nodded when Kaelii put the question to him.

"Good," Len said.

"What if the folk here are brave and will not move?" asked Madrra, chief of the Bone Jackals. Her eyes and mouth were perpetually askance. *Like she was born doubtful.*

"The valley-folk are simple and strange–more than me," he answered in her tongue. That earned him a chuckle from Dubrhos. "They run in terror. All they leave is yours."

"What if a few do not run?" she pressed.

A vision of Young Beard shimmered in Len's mind. "No spill blood!" he came back, more adamant. "There is time for–" *What's their word for it?*"For wrath. But no wrath betwixt human-folk today."

He reverted to his own speech. "Any Child of Dust who draws the strangers' blood, excepting in his own defense, will be punished."

Kaelii translated. Fear shone in the chiefs' faces. *Healthy fear.* Under the sun's glare, Len couldn't tell whether Egwae wore a smirk or a grimace. "Let your clan-folk know these things," he told the chiefs. They dispersed to their clans to relay his instructions.

He wasn't the only one to note the warden's expression. "Why she look you this way?" Kaelii inquired.

Len's world came to a standstill. His mind grasped for a fitting response, to no avail.

Impatient, Kaelii turned to Egwae. "Why you smile strange at Len?"

The warden had no trouble finding words. "The wanderer lets not bloodshed stand betwixt him and what he desires."

"What she talk about? You hurt folk?"

"No! Not–on purpose," he stammered.

"Who hurt?" Kaelii asked him. "Who hurt to get what want?"

Who haven't I hurt? The answer eluded him.

"You hurt folk here? Want us hurt them?" Her hackles were up. "Like your fire-spirit hurt us folk afore?"

Len's mouth worked, but naught came out. He watched Kaelii's desert-wrought face change to stone. She turned Rabbit and started north along the ridge.

"Kaelii!" *Don't go.* She didn't slow or look back.

He rounded on Egwae. "Look what you've done!" he accosted her. "That wasn't your place!"

"What *I* have done?" she asked. *That's a smirk she's wearing now, for sure.*

"Get away from me, demon," he spat, full of loathing. "For that's all you are."

Egwae seemed bored. Or distracted. Her eyes kept darting to the north. "As it happens, briefly must I tend to something else. Others than you lay schemes, now and again."

After all this time, she has other affairs to tend? He wouldn't protest, but he was leery. "Then good riddance. If only briefly." *However long that is to her kind.*

"From a distance will I keep watch, fear not," Egwae said drily. She began walking the same way as Kaelii and Rabbit. "And watch on her shall I also keep, if I can," she added in parting.

That wasn't like her in the slightest. The warden had lost her senses. *Of all the moments for her to interfere. Of all the days for her to open her mouth!*

Big Len scuffed the ground. It brought him back to his surroundings. *There's no more time to fret about Egwae. And I'll have to sort things out later with Kaelii. If I can find her.* The Children of Dust stood prepared. Kræwk and his Camel Lords waited in position above him. "Wanderer!" the chief hailed him. "Your folk are ready!"

"Then down we go," Len called back in his own tongue. "Children of Dust, with me!"

A few excitable heart-thuds later, Kræwk and the other chiefs had their clans moving. The desert-folk, with shrill whoops and hollers, surged over the ridge. Len turned Big Len west once more and let him have free rein. Together he and his folk commenced the long, gentle descent into the valley.

Soon a dozen or so of the greater camels raced ahead of their fellow hump-backs. These Camel Lords, Kræwk among them as always, loped abreast of Big Len to either side. The rest of the Children of Dust flanked Len and his escort in a loose, shifting order. A glance over his shoulder, through dust clouds the beasts kicked up, showed Kaelii and Rabbit watching from the next rise over. *Watching me.* Of Egwae there was no sign.

The stone-beast's bulk lent them speed as they careened toward the river. Len let his soul revel in the exhilaration. Cool wind off the Fangs, and the overwhelming greenness lying before them, removed all distractions and reservations. *I want to taste berries. I want to bathe in streams. Mayhap I can't plant and harvest, but the Wright won't stop me from watching green things grow.* For a passing instant, he imagined well-tended gardens and groves stretching the whole length of the valley.

Afore he knew it, they'd reached the bow of the river. Big Len slowed, and Len let him munch on a willow tree by the bank. He fancied it was Egwae. *What's she up to?* It was both blissful and unsettling to be spared the warden's presence. *And where is Kaelii now?*

The Camel Lords were allowing their mounts to nibble on tree foliage, too. Len caught Kræwk's attention. "Find spots where the water is not deep," he called to the chief. "So folk on small beasts can cross easy." Kræwk nodded understanding and issued a series of sharp commands to the other men-folk.

Shortly, the riders from the other clans caught up. Len watched them begin to ford the river on their lesser camels. The water made him think of the sky, if sky were more alive, flowing and burbling. *I reckon Kaelii would say the sky is plenty alive. That it whispers to us.*

When the stone-beast eased into the river up to his knees to drink, Len plucked a round, fat fruit from a branch overhanging the bank. *I don't know this kind.* It was pale red. He tore into its flesh with his teeth and found it tasty. *Almost honeyish.* For a spell, he ignored as best he could the clamor of the caravan crossing the river. He snacked on the fruit and watched the current for swirls and eddies. A silvery critter broke the surface. *Fish. Not one of Livyat's spawn.* Leastways, he didn't think so. Yet he got the creeping feeling that the water was watching back.

Then Kræwk's voice interrupted his respite. "We wish to claim our land now." The Camel Lord chief and his family awaited Len's answer from the far bank. His young son's head spun from one brilliant diversion to the next, as if the boy had ventured into the heaven-realm. *It's a wonder his little hat stays put.*

Len nodded. "Of course. First things afore others." The first clan to join him ought to have opportunity to claim the territory most to their liking.

Kræwk frowned. *He's uncomprehending.* "Go ahead," Len said in Kræwk's speech. "Camel Lords are lords of the valley." He grinned.

The chief grunted and dipped his head. "You keep your promises, wanderer." After a few words exchanged with his wife, he moved off to wrangle his clan-folk.

Len decided to take Big Len across the river and accompany the Camel Lords. Like a little flood, the Children of Dust were pouring onto the grassy plain north and west of the river crossing. They skirted the occasional tree-stand or thicket and kept to the open space, of which there was plenty. *I sure wish Kaelii were here.*

He stuck close to Kræwk but allowed the chief to lead the way. They hugged the tree-lined river on its diversion north toward the Fangs, afore it resumed its easterly course. The chief explained to Len, "This is beautiful, strange country. Better than the wastes. But we must not stray far from the sand. That is where our camels belong." It had scarcely occurred to Len that some of the desert-folk might miss the wastes after leaving. *Will Kaelii pine for the dunes? So far as I know, she's gone back to them already.*

They neared the shallow-looking spot where the river started to veer east again. It bypassed the foothills and flowed into the wastes, where it dwindled and vanished. Except for trees along the riverbanks, there was naught taller than a shrub within a thousand paces. Kræwk raised a hand to halt their party. "Here," he said, and used his arm to indicate a broad swathe of bottomland, mostly level, along the river. The Camel Lords cheered.

Len eyed the clump of hills he'd pointed out to the chiefs earlier. It was situated slightly north and a ways west of where they stood now, even closer to the great Fang looming above. *That's for Morii's folk, if they and their poky aurochses ever make it that far. The Stone Pickers can build houses there for all the clans.* It would be the center of their new realm. Mayhap there'd be a stone house for him, too, thereabouts. *For us?* If he had children someday, it was where he supposed they ought to enter the earthly realm. *Up in the Fangs. Same as me.*

He said to Kræwk in desert speech, "I look in hills now, afore Stone Pickers come. You send few Camel Lords with me? Others stay with you. Make camp."

The chief began shouting names. Half his men-folk, nearly two dozen, unloaded their families and baggage at the river to ride with Len. The other half took charge of the camels and kept wary eyes on their new environs, while the women-folk set up the tents and the young ones played. Kræwk's handpicked contingent of Camel Lords gathered shortly–the chief among them. Each carried a stone-tipped hunting spear.

"Much obliged," Len said to Kræwk.

"We keep our promises, too," he replied.

Big Len wanted to eat again, but Len used the reins and his boots to prompt the stone-beast toward the group of hills. "You're living in plenty now. Like the rest of us." *No need to bust his stomach at every opportunity. He's a big enough critter as is.*

Their reduced company passed by a few abandoned campsites in various states of disarray. Halfway to their destination, he noticed a line of hillocks where somebody had dug holes into the short slopes. *They're houses. In the ground?* Intrigued though he was, he signaled to Kræwk not to stray any closer. *If any barbarians are hiding there, I'd rather not find out yet.* Kræwk's eyes didn't leave the hillside holes till they passed out of sight. He'd be back here later, no matter what Len said.

Once they got within a few thousand paces, they could see disordered droves of barbarians spread across the hillsides. They were fleeing west. *From us. They reckon we're the barbarians.* At a thousand paces, a loose knot of some three dozen men-folk started their way. When Len saw they carried crude clubs and rocks, he motioned to Kræwk to halt. The chief told his Camel Lords to form a line and await the valley-folk.

"Do not hurt them," Len warned his escort in their tongue. Kræwk looked mildly insulted that he'd felt the need to repeat his earlier instruction. The others nodded gravely, without taking their eyes off the fool barbarians. Len walked the stone-beast back several paces, behind the camels. *I don't want to look the coward. But the safer I am, the less likely the warden will show up.* The last thing he wanted was Egwae's help inaugurating his return with another bloodbath.

The barbarians slowed to a creep a fair distance off. *They're realizing in full just how massive the Camel Lords' beasts are.* Kræwk's face was so tense, the wind off the Fangs seemed liable to crack it. The other desert-folk wore grim expressions.

Len didn't see which barbarian threw the first rock. Kræwk's camel grunted in pain as the missile struck it in the nose. "No!" Len protested. More rocks flew. The camels were riled and scared, and their riders struggled to hold the line. *Aught but this. Not again.* Len's men either had to advance or flee. *I said I'd keep them safe.* "Let's go! Run!" he shouted to Kræwk. But it was too late. The Camel Lords were too proud to turn tail when they stood betwixt Len and danger. They charged.

The barbarians scattered in every direction. At least half were trampled anyway; their screams sufficed to curdle blood. Len kept a tight rein on Big Len and bit back tears. *I'm cursed. I'm truly cursed.*

One of the desert-folk nearest him had a nasty-looking gash on his head. A tall barbarian wearing a too-tight tunic grabbed the Camel Lord by the leg and pulled him from his mount. Together the men tumbled to the ground, flailing and striking each other in frenzied fashion. By happenchance, afore anyone else could intervene, the Camel Lord struck the barbarian's throat with his elbow. That ended the tussle. The enraged Camel Lord seized the hapless barbarian by the shoulders and slammed his broad-shouldered back against the ground, over and over.

The brawl awakened a memory. Len knew that anger, the burning beyond control. “Stop!” he yelled in desert speech. He urged Big Len into the fray. *Protect them!*

Oblivious to Len’s pleas, the Camel Lord smashed the other man’s great-bearded head into the earth. Len gagged. The juice of the fruit he’d eaten rose in his throat like a stream overflowing its banks. *Kaelii had the right of it. Look what I’ve done.* He felt numb.

Kræwk rode up, cursing his clansman, who looked agape at the blood on his hands. Someone shouted in Len’s tongue. *It’s me.* His voice was dampened in his ears, as if he were submerged in water or caught in a furious wind. “Into the desert!” he said again.

The chief on his mount and the other Camel Lord both looked at him uncertainly. *Where did that notion come from?* But it seemed right to him. Len said in their speech, “Go to desert. You take life, you walk to wastes. Wander by lonesome all days under sun.” Kræwk grimaced but gave his customary, solemn nod. He muttered stern words to the dumbfounded man kneeling over the dead barbarian.

Len didn’t linger. He couldn’t look at that lifeless body another moment. He became aware, too, of the other valley-folk who hadn’t run or limped off. Some moaned while others lay still. “Help if can,” he said loudly, in desert speech, to nobody in particular. He couldn’t think straight.

Livyat take me. Even without the warden, I sow destruction. He wanted his Children of Dust to flout his curse and spite the heaven-realm by flourishing here. *I want the Wright to see my folk grow like a garden.* Violence and bloodshed would only uproot. That wasn't the story he wanted any child of his born into.

Afeared he'd topple off the stone-beast in his befuddlement, Len clicked his tongue thrice. Big Len sank to the ground to let him dismount. He felt a touch steadier once his boots hit the waist-high grass. *When's the last time I stood on earth so solid?* He patted the beast's leg. *Let him graze for a bit.* There were no barbarians for a thousand paces who could threaten them.

A pair of giant camels walked toward him. He couldn't tell if the riders were looking for instruction or wondering if he needed help. Either way, he waved them off. "Tell Kræwk, wait here for Stone Pickers," he said. *I need to sort myself out.*

Chapter Twelve:
PLAYING WITH SERPENTS

Len wandered a bit, aimless. When a wind blew down from the mountain, he tensed, expectant and listening. But it was a mundane kind of wind. It carried no voice; it only rippled the yellow-green grass. *The Wright has naught to say to me. Well, I've naught to say, either, just now.*

Soon he happened on a dip in the earth where the grass had hidden a narrow creek from view. It chattered cheerily. Len knelt to splash water on his face. Past the drip from his brow and lashes, he noticed an object flattening some grass on the other side of the creek. He rose to his feet and waded across. *Not possible.*

Lying in the grass was a flat length of stone, familiar in its contours. *Memory's an odd thing. But it's uncanny.* He could swear it was identical to the stone blade he'd carried down the Fangs upon a time. *Not identical–the same.* Yet he'd discarded the blade to follow Egwae into the wastes. *This isn't the spot I left it, either–not even close.* He balanced the stone in his palm and pondered.

A shivery, crawling sensation raised the hairs on his back, up to the nape of his neck. From behind came a rasping whisper, bestial and vaguely feminine. “You are the hope.”

Len spun and looked for the serpentine critter he’d seen at the watering hole. Naught moved but the grass in the breeze.

“You are the hope of man,” the voice said. *It’s coming from the creek.*

“Who are you?” he demanded. He was unsure where to direct his question. Instead of a reply, he heard a splash upstream. There he saw the last thing he expected.

The man at the creekside was dressed in a cloak and britches similar to Len’s. But this fellow wasn’t shaggy or sunbaked. There was a brightness about his features, and his eyes were hazel. *The dawn-break child.*

It was Sceg. Len was looking at his brother. Leastways, it was an apparition of his brother. They traded gazes. In his gut, Len knew this wasn’t right. *This can’t be Sceg–not truly.* He sensed something slippery and false. It felt like he was staring at that servant of Livyat by the oasis.

All the same, Len couldn’t hold back the words. “I’m sorry.”

Sceg who wasn’t Sceg turned and walked away north, toward the foothills. Len hastened after him. A tickle in the back of his mind kept him from dropping the stone blade where he’d found it. “Did you hear?” he called out. “I’m sorry, I said!”

Though he didn't answer, Sceg walked faster. So Len walked faster. Sceg began running, and Len ran after him. "Stop!" he shouted. "Who are you?" Sceg never broke stride. Len kept up his pursuit across uneven ground, leaping over small juts of rock.

Whoever this Sceg was, he was getting Len's dander up. *Is it a demon in Sceg's guise?* He could be chasing a mirage some fell spirit imposed on his mind. If it were his brother for true, Len was at a greater loss. *How? Mayhap he's a spirit now. Beholden to unseen powers. To Livyat–because of how he died?*

The chase led Len betwixt stands of trees, through a thicket, and up a hillock. His feet didn't so much mind the boots now. *I ought to thank Kaelii after this.* The demon, if that's what this Sceg was, didn't stop till reaching the top of the little hill. Sceg turned about. His hazel eyes were cold, yet seeing. Len halted, too, half a dozen paces behind.

"Forgive me," Len pled. *It doesn't stand to reason, wanting forgiveness from this thing.* But he wasn't of a mind to heed reason just now.

With hands and fingers crooked like claws, Sceg snarled and lunged at Len. Every inclination of Len's mind resisted his body's itch to defend itself. *Never again. Not with him.* He wanted all this to prove an unpleasant dream. Or a jest, like when they were young and running about the hollow together. If naught else, he wanted to fade into air and drift away on a wind afore Sceg could reach him.

Yet none of those things happened. Instead, self-preservation took hold of Len. He raised the stone blade high. Sceg's distorted countenance looked violence at him. *It's not my brother.* Len squeezed his eyes shut at the last instant and swung his weapon in a downward arc at the demon's shoulder.

The stone blade didn't connect with flesh or bone. Len lost his hat but narrowly kept his feet at their collision. His eyes opened wide to see that the demon gripped both the wrist and bicep of Len's blade arm. They grappled in a desperate embrace, shifting and scraping for the slightest advantage. Len's heartbeat pounded in his ears.

This isn't like the other times we've tussled. Len had always been a bit bigger and more solidly wrought, which lent him the edge in any scrap. This demon in Sceg's form proved stronger than Len and seemed intent on grinding him into the hillside. Already Len's limbs strained; he struggled not to be overpowered. *Where's Egwae gone to?*

Len's right boot slid on a patch of loose earth where their scuffle had torn up the grass. The demon wrested the stone blade from him and threw him bodily to the ground. It didn't speak, but it gave Len an unblinking stare and a cruel, serpentine smile. The expression both mesmerized Len and angrified him. *It doesn't belong on my brother's face.*

The demon raised the flat length of stone across its chest, poised to smite Len's head with a backhanded stroke. Len readied his forearms to fend off the blow, though they'd likely shatter in the effort.

Then the demon froze, without so much as a twitch in its stare or its sickly smile. "Your kind is broken," hissed the feminine voice he'd heard afore. "Serve me and I will give you and yours power–over forest and mountain and sea. Simply allow me to mark you as mine. 'Tis the only hope for the earthly realm."

Len remembered the desert-folk he'd adopted and remade in his likeness. He thought of his children unborn. *They need safekeeping. And hope. I was wrought for that purpose. I can do what's required.* His lips trembled as they formed an answer.

Then he recalled one other soul. *Kaelii. Strong and stubborn. Wind and dust.* His reply to the Mother of Serpents changed somewhere betwixt his mind and his mouth.

Just afore Len spoke, the demon's eyes darted up and fixed somewhere past Len. It tossed the stone blade aside and dropped to the grass beside Len, splaying its arms and legs like a lizard. The demon flashed Len a last look of cold malice and skittered over the hilltop on hands and feet, with bewildering speed.

I'm losing my senses. Len let himself collapse fully on his back with his head turned up to the Fangs. He gazed absently at the forested heights over the foothills. Exhaustion weighed on him like a mountain. "Mayhap not today," he murmured, "but one day soon, I'm headed up that slope. I'm coming for you." He wasn't sure what soul or spirit he spoke to. More than aught else, he craved rest with a vengeance.

He let the Fang above flood his vision and noticed its snowcap had turned bloody red. The snow thawed afore his eyes. Liquid fireblooms poured down the mountainside. *It's only a vision.* Yet it was terrible to behold.

Then red waves crashed over the hills and surged toward him as he lay helpless. *Mayhap it's real.* It was a frightful notion, but he lacked the will to stir himself. *If it's not a dream, and I drown in bloody blossoms in a few moments' time, so be it.* Kaelii would be safe in the wastes, and Len would finally have peace. *But I'll miss her.*

There was someone behind him. A distinctive shadow partly blocked the early afternoon sun.

"You truly are my warden," Len said with a wry, croaking laugh. "Warding off Livyat's spawn just by showing up." *Mayhap she's kept them at bay all this while. Till today.*

"A fool are you, son of Ghrem," Egwae's voice replied. *Is that a note of relief, or my imagining?* Two slender hands hauled him upright with disproportionate strength. His head lolled a moment, and his knees and booted feet threatened to buckle under him. Then a stinging slap across the cheek brought him to. His joints ceased their wobbling, and his legs held his weight. Grey-green clouds roiled in Egwae's eyes as she looked hard into his.

"I said, a fool are you, Ghrem-son, like your father and mother afore you," she spat. "Intent are you and your ilk, every dust-coated soul, on doing as you were not meant to do. Going where forbidden. Refusing to be content with more than you deserve."

"Egwae–"

She didn't let up. "A noble existence had I once. Thanks to you and your kin, relegated am I to watchkeeper of two-legged children. And still are you bent on playing with serpents." She sneered. "Let the snakes have you, too, I would. The cause of my misery are you, but my failure will you not become."

When she finished her rant, he began to chortle. From the depths of his soul, he laughed and kept laughing. Mirth made his stomach ache, but it took the edge off his weariness. *I don't hate her anymore. I pity her.*

In disgust, Egwae turned and walked past him, down the side of the hillock. It seemed they'd both been bound to the Wright's whims. *But no longer. Leastways, not me. Let the sky-lord have his realm, and the Mother of Serpents hers. I want neither. This earthly realm is for me and mine.*

"No be mad at Egwae. No her fault." Len almost fell again, so quick did he turn about. *She's here.* Kaelii held his hat and fixed him with a weighing look. "She is what she made be, yes? And she say, Len need help. I come." She paused expectantly.

"I'm sorry," Len said simply.

She nodded, her face still as stony as when she'd left him on the ridge.

He breathed deep. "I need to tell you about my brother."

Her green eyes made the valley look like the wastes. "It is complicated, I think. Later we talk."

Len pondered a moment. "Yes," he said, switching to the desert speech. "Later we talk much. And after, we build a stone house."

Her countenance melted and left behind a desert rose. *My desert rose, mayhap.* This time when she nodded, her eyes misted and a tear trickled down her cheek. "Okay, mate." She closed the space betwixt them, looking solemn. "We build a house. You and me."

Afore he could stop her, she reached up ran a finger along the lines of raised flesh on his brow. Len winced. Then his eyes widened. Her touch soothed his mark like it wasn't even there. He let himself relax. Kaelii smiled gently. When she withdrew her hand, she stood on her tiptoes and set his hat upon his head. He smiled back. A soft light blossomed in his heart.

"Well then," he said, reverting to his own tongue, "we'd best get going." Looking about, he saw Egwae at the bottom of the hillock, but no Rabbit. "Kaelii, how did Egwae get you get here so quick?"

She shrugged. "Tell you later. It is complicated."

Fair enough. He placed an arm around her shoulders. Together they looked out over the valley. Betwixt the Fangs and the bow of the river, the Children of Dust scurried to and fro. "We have a new realm in the making," he said quietly. "And we don't need fire-spirits or the Wright above or serpents below to do it."

She rested her cheek against the goat-hair covering his arm. "Fight spirits up high and snakes down low? Too many. They break us in middle. We pick one or other, mayhap."

Len grunted and considered what she'd said. "I reckon I pick you."

Kaelii snorted laughter. "Time is a-wasting, mate."

It doesn't feel like wasting time. But he didn't care to argue. Together they made their way downhill, hand in hand.

ACKNOWLEDGMENTS

I owe debts of gratitude to my wife and family for their unconditional love, grace, forbearance, encouragement, prayer, and provision of physical sustenance. This book is, in a real sense, as much yours as mine.

Kids, when you start reading (any day now, I'm sure), know that your imminent arrival kept the fire lit under your dad's rear to finish this story. Neither the first draft nor my learning process was pretty, but your mama is an epically tough (and sweet) cookie.

Thanks to my brother for helping me build this story-world. That's still the most fun part.

To my sister and other stalwart Substack readers, I owe thanks for timely encouragement and for patience with wordy, convoluted, plot-hole-pocked drafts. Because of y'all, I've had the space to sort out what I'm doing.

Thank you, Word Menders and other Realmies, for the community, inspiration, and gentle yet apt criticism you've provided.

And thanks to Four Star for assisting with the print run for events..

I truly appreciate all my friends, kin, and colleagues for cheering me on. It's been a humbling journey in every respect.